To Save Michael

To Save Michael

Nicole Kinney

Library of Congress Control Number: 2019902495
ISBN: Hardcover   978-1-7960-1926-1
                   Softcover   978-1-7960-1927-8
                   eBook   978-1-7960-1928-5

Print information available on the last page.

Rev. date: 02/28/2019

To order additional copies of this book, contact:
Xlibris
1-888-795-4274
www.Xlibris.com
Orders@Xlibris.com
793207

To my older brother Michael,

Thank you for always being there for me. Thank you
for believing in me and believing that I can do this even
when I didn't believe it myself. This book is for you.

I love you. Always.

Contents

CHAPTER 1

Michael

INEVER THOUGHT FINDING certain people would be so hard. I've been searching for over two months for people with superhuman powers and I haven't found one. Right now, I'm passing through Jamestown, New York. A town that isn't much. Miles from any amusement park or beach. There is a mall in the next small town over where pretty much all the major food product stores were. The mall was small, but at least it was something. There has got to be no way I'd find somebody here. This town was way too small to find someone.

I checked in at a hotel and decided that I'd wander the town. I bought a map of the town from the hotel gift shop to help me as I walk around. It was getting dark and although the hotel manager whose name I didn't catch said Jamestown was bad at night and that I should wait until the morning, I still left the hotel with the map in my hands.

I have been walking around for an hour. The hotel manager was right, Jamestown is bad at night. I have seen drunks get into fights with other drunks. People trying to break into places like homes and abandoned buildings. I've seen some sad things as well. Like families living out on the street. I gave some money to some small families I saw. I sighed. Exhausted, I was about to go back to the hotel and give up for the night when I stopped. Standing on a corner was a teenager. He looked like he was about sixteen or maybe seventeen. He had dark hair and looked like he was six feet tall or maybe taller. It was eleven at night so what would he be doing out here alone this late? He looked like he was waiting for someone, but he also looked scared. Like something could be bothering him. He didn't even seem to notice me standing a few feet away. After a few minutes of watching the teenager, a man in a very nice suit walked by the teenager. I didn't think anything of it until the teenager followed behind the nice suited man. Something sparked my curiosity, so I followed. I walked close enough not to lose them, but far enough away that they would not see me or notice I was following them. They turned into an alley that had a dead-end sign. I followed into the alley and crouched behind a nearby dumpster for a restaurant nearby. The teenager stood in front of the man in a stance like he was making sure he can't go anywhere. The man was against the wall behind him and he was now the one looking scared. They looked like a car catching its prey and the teenager was the cat.

"Where is the money?" the teenager asked in a demanding tone. Was the teenager really shaking a grown man down for money?

"I-I d-don't h-have I-it." The man stuttered to say. The teenager looked at the man. I watched as the man lifted into the air. I put my hand over my mouth to cover up any noise so I couldn't be heard. "P-please. I-I-I'll g-get the m-money. J-Just let l-let m-me d-down," the man said.

"You owe D six grand. Your pay was due a week ago. He will not like it if I come back empty handed." The teenager said, stepping closer to the man. I realized that it was the teenager keeping the man in the air. The fact that he wasn't touching him sparked my attention even more.

"I-I'll g-get the m-money. I-I swear." The guy said. The teenager sighed before the man fell to the ground. He stumbled when he stood up and his suit was messed up and dirty. He took off and ran out of the alley as fast as he could. The teenager stood there for a moment before walking away. I leaned out of the way, hoping not to be spotted. As soon he was gone and the coast was clear I got up and followed him. He walked through town like what just happened didn't actually happen. No one he walked by said anything to him or even acted as they noticed him. I watched him walk right into a bar without the bouncer even looking at him. How is that possible? Maybe he didn't see the teenager or maybe the bouncer was here for people who got into fights and not to stop people from going in. I walked up to the bar ready to just walk in just like the teenager, but I got stopped by the bouncer before I could enter.

"ID please." The bouncer said. He was a beefy man who looked like he could bench press two of me.

"You just let that teenager in without asking him for his ID." I said. The bouncer looked behind him before looking back at me.

"What teenager?" the bouncer asked. "ID or you're not getting in." I rolled my eyes and pulled my wallet out to show the bouncer my ID. He nodded and I went inside. It was crowded so he was hard to find at first, but I found him walking to the far corner of the bar. He sat down in a booth that had an empty booth in front of it. I quickly took the empty booth before someone else could. I ordered a beer while I watched and waited. I watched as the teenager also ordered a beer. The bartender brought him one, but the beer just sat on his table. He didn't drink any of it which surprised me after what I saw him do to the man in the alley. The kid had to be a drinker if he could do that. I know I would.

Three in the morning, the bar was almost empty. We've been sitting here for almost four hours and the teenager never moved. The beer was still on the table, never touched. Probably warm by now. Nothing was happening so I was about to give up and leave when someone walked into the bar. The place was practically empty. The only people here now were the bartender, the bouncer, the teenager, and me so why was someone walking into the bar at this hour? A few people walked in behind him. I watched as they all walked up to the teenager waiting at the booth.

"Where is my money?" the guy asked in a rude tone.

"I don't have it," the teenager said, looking down. The guy looked disappointed and mad. "I didn't get it from him. I'm sorry, but he didn't have the money. None of it."

"You only have one job to do! Get me my money! How hard is it to do one damn job!" the guy shouted. "It's a simple damn job!"

"I'm not your dang monkey! If you want your money then you go get your money yourself!" the teenager snapped, standing up and facing the guy.

"What was that?!" the guy asked. He rose his hand. His hand flung forward and the next thing I knew the teenager was on the floor with his face bloody. "Never say that to me again! Get me my money!" He demanded and walked away without another word to the teenager. I quickly got out of my booth and went over to the teenager.

"Are you alright?" I asked. I looked at his face. He was bleeding from his upper lip. I tried to touch his lip, but he pushed me away.

"I'm fine lady." The teenager said. He got up and stormed out. Something was not right. I got up and followed him out of the bar and onto the street.

I walked slowly behind him. I need to know where he was going. I followed him as he went down alley after alley, ignoring all the main roads. It was like he was trying to hide from someone. I followed until he got to a house outside of town. He looked around behind going to an open window. He quickly climbed in and headed inside. There was probably nothing else I can do tonight so I decided to go back to the hotel and find him again in the morning. How hard will that be? I just have to remember where this house is. It shouldn't be that hard.

I slowly walked away from the house, making sure I'm not caught by him or by anyone. I walked away from the house a little before turning around and looking back at the house. It looked blue not that you could really tell. It looked like the house hasn't been worked on in years. Windows upstairs looked broken and roof tiles were falling to the yard. It was not a house people should live in so why was he going in?

I walked back to the hotel. As the hotel came into view, I heard footsteps behind me. I looked back to see no one there, making me walk faster. I got to the hotel and looked behind me. No one was still there. Maybe I'm losing my mind due to exhaustion.

"Are you alright ma'am?" the manager asked, making me jump. I put my hand over my chest to calm myself. "I'm so sorry. I didn't mean to startle you."

"No, it's okay." I said. "I didn't hear you come up to me and I just thought someone was following me, but maybe it was just in my head."

"Why don't I walk you to your room?" he offered. I smiled at him and nodded.

"That would be great." I said. We started walking towards the elevator. I was shaking. If someone was following me, I didn't know who would, but it probably has something to do with what I saw tonight. We got to the elevator and we walked in. He pressed the button for the right floor. Everything was silent as the elevator went up. Not the good kind of silent. It was awkward and weird. The manager kept looking at me like he wanted to say something, but he just kept quiet. The elevator made a noise and the doors opened. I started walking towards my room as I pulled out my room key, but the manager grabbed me and pulled me away from the door.

"I'm sorry, but I can't do this," he said. I looked at him confused. What was that supposed to mean?

"Can't do what?" I asked as he pulled me the opposite direction of my room. We went to a room at the other end of the hall. He pulled out a new room key and took the one I had away. "What's going on? Why are you giving me a different room? I already have one."

"Please tell me that you weren't near Michael tonight?" he asked.

"So, that's his name." I said. "I thought I saw something." I shrugged and we went inside the new room.

"No, you saw something." He corrected me. "Someone very powerful in this town holds that boy and gets rid of anyone that gets in his way. I don't want that happening to you."

"What if I told you that I can save Michael?" I asked.

"Are you insane?! He sent men here just for following Michael!" he said. "I told them you were in your room all night and it couldn't possibly be you."

"I really can help him though." I said. He sighed. "I just need a little bit of time to prove it."

"Don't leave this room until morning." He ordered. "If anyone asks you were in this room all night." I nodded and he left the room. I went to the bed and laid down, letting exhaustion take over and falling right to sleep.

I woke up to the sun hitting my face from the window. I sat up in my bed and looked around. At first, I was confused onto why I wasn't in my room, but then I remembered what happened last night when I got back to the hotel. I got out of bed and quickly went to the door. I opened the door and saw two guys standing in the hallway near my old door. My eyes landed on something on both waists. Their guns. I shut the door before they could notice me. I know I needed to get past the men and get out of this hotel to find Michael. Something about him and the bad guy makes me want to help, not just about the power I witnessed.

I didn't have my suitcase. That was in the room they are guarding. All I had was the clothes I was still wearing. I took the flannel top and tied it around my waist, leaving my undershirt on. I also managed to find a pair of scissors in the kitchen. I cut my pants into shorts. Lastly, I put my hair into a ponytail and hopefully made it so I didn't look like I was the one that stalked Michael last night. I took a deep breath and opened the door. Three more have joined them in the hallway since I opened the door a few minutes ago. I recognized them all from the bar last night. They looked more like goons from here. They all stood in attention as soon as I was in the hallway. My eyes went to the magnum .357 attached to their waists. I quietly walked to the elevator. I thought for a second that I was in the clear until I heard a voice from one of them.

"Have you seen the woman that is supposed to be staying in this room?" one of them asked, pointing to my original room. The goon was twice my size.

"No, I'm sorry. I haven't seen her." I said, I pushed the button for the ground floor. I smiled and waved at the goons. Their eyes practically popped out of their sockets and I knew I was caught. A hand flew in between the doors, stopping the elevator from closing and made it open again. I looked to see them all staring at me. Their expressions are a mix between surprised and mad.

"You need to come with us," the one that first spoke said in a demanding tone.

"I would, but I don't want to." I said, backing up until my back hit the back wall of the elevator.

"I don't think you understand me. I never said you had a choice," he said in a rude tone.

"I don't think you understand. I never said I was letting you take me." I said. I did the first thing that came to mind. I hit my foot as hard as I could into the goon's stomach, making him tumble back into the others like dominos. They all fell back and I ran out of the elevator and down the hall. The door marked *stairway* was my new exit. I didn't have another place to go with them all in the doorway of the elevator. I opened the door ready to run, but before I went through I stopped and looked back at the goons. I caught one of them close to me. I felt the sharp pain of the wall hitting my side as he kicked me hard. I fell down the stairs. I quickly got up before any of them could come down the stairs and catch up with me. I limped the rest of the way back down the stairs, going to the basement where the workers get ready for their shifts. I went all the way to the back where giant washers and dryers were kept. I hid in the small corner where hopefully no one could see me and waited. A few minutes later I heard footsteps and voices. It was mainly the one that spoke to me first while upstairs.

"Find her. She is hurt so she couldn't have gotten far," he said. It went quiet and I thought they all left and I was about to move until I heard a phone go off and then his voice again so I stayed where I was and listened. "D. No, she got away. Don't worry she got injured so if she goes to a hospital we will know. We'll find her. I promise." It went quiet for a moment as he listened to whoever was on the other end. "We'll go get him." I heard footsteps walk away as he left.

Things just got together.

I waited there until I knew it was safe. I painfully stood up and moved from where I was hiding. I walked out of the room and down the hall. I walked out of the employee entrance of the hotel and into the fresh air. I had to find some place to get looked at, but after what he said I knew the hospital was out. Maybe the manager that helped me last night could know someone that will help me. Ignoring the voice in my head telling me going back is a bad idea and that I could probably get myself killed, I went back to the door I came out of and slipped back in. Not trusting the elevator, I went back to the door marked *stairway*. I looked up the stairs. No one looked like they were on the stairs so I quietly walking up the stairs, checking everywhere before going up each staircase.

I made it up the stairs without a problem. The problem started when I got to the top of the stairs. I went to the lobby looking for the manager. That is when my problem really started. The lobby was surrounded by goons. No one noticed yet. I looked around the lobby and someone caught my attention.

Michael. He is here.

He stood next to the goon from the elevator. I really should get his name. Michael was looking around at everyone. His eyes spotted me. They opened wide. I put my fingers to my lips. He shook his head at me like he was trying to tell me not to do it. Luckily no one saw him. I looked around again. There must be something that could help me. My breath hitched as a goon walked by me. I released it when he kept walking. I don't think he knew what I looked like or else he would have stopped me. Not watching where I was going I walked right into a side table and knocked a vase over. It broke loudly into pieces, making all eyes on me. I mentally slapped myself.

"GET HER!" the goon by Michael yelled and everyone started to move. The next thing I knew I was dodging people. I slid between someone's legs and got up. Michael was pushed to the wall with two goons standing in front of him, guarding him. Their guns now in their hands. I looked around. There were hotel guests screaming and running away as goons were running towards me. I ran over to the front desk. I jumped up on it. They all stopped running and looked at me. "What are you waiting for?! Don't just stand there! GO!" he shouted. I jumped behind the front desk, trying to find a place to hide. The only place I could hide was under the desk, but the space was too small. I was shocked when everyone was lifted into the air and thrown into walls without being touched. I looked at Michael. I could see the anger in his eyes. I quickly got out from behind the front desk.

"Listen to me." I said as I walked over to Michael. He was still starting at the people hanging on the walls. "Michael!" He finally looking at me. "Listen to me. They are going to take you and try to make sure I can't find you, but I promise you I will. You just have to trust me." Michael stared at me for a moment then I heard a huge crash and multiple groans. Michael looked from me to someone behind me.

"DON'T HURT HER!" Michael shouted as someone grabbed me from behind. I didn't turn around to see who it was that grabbed me. "I'll come with you just don't hurt her." Michael pleaded. I was let go and Michael was taken out of here. I stood there long after they were gone. Not moving, just staring at the door. I knew not to go after them especially not in this condition.

"You should get that looked at," someone said. I turned around to see the manager standing there. His hands were in his pockets.

"They are watching the hospital. If I go there I'll be screwed." I said.

"Come with me," he said. I followed him outside to an old red car in the parking lot. He got in and I just stood outside, not sure what to do or if I can trust him. I know I was looking for him, but now I'm not so sure. "Well, come on." I sighed and got into the car then he drove off.

"Where are you taking me?" I asked. He looked at me and then back to the road.

"I have a friend who can look at you," he said.

"But I can't go to the hospital." I pointed out. "They'll capture me."

"He doesn't work at the hospital anymore. He's retired. He is a great doctor. He'll be able to fix you right up," the manager said. I just sat back in the seat of the car. Can I trust this other guy? Will he really help me or rat me out to those goons? "We're here." I looked to see that we were parked in front of an old house in the middle of town.

"You have got to be kidding me." I said. It was an old house sitting between buildings that looked like they were recently built. We got out. I walked behind him. I looked around as we walked. We could have been followed, but there was no one on the street, not even a car. So maybe we're safe for now. "I didn't learn your name. You're helping me and I don't even know your name." I said.

"Jerry Andrews," he said, smiling at me.

"Nicole. Nicole Sullivan." I said. He knocked on a door. A few minutes later someone opened the door. It was a man. He looked to be in his mid-eighties maybe nineties.

"Jerry," the man at the door said, smiling at him once he realized who it was.

"Arthur." Jerry replied. "It's nice to see you. I need a favor, can we come in?" Jerry asked, gesturing to him and myself.

"Sure. Come in, come in." the man Jerry named Arthur said. He moved aside and we walked in. "What's the reason for this visit?"

"I have this problem." I spoke up. He looked at me and nodded to keep talking. "I am trying to help this teenager and it takes more than what I though and I ended up injured." I pulled up my shirt to reveal the wound on my side. I watched their faces as they looked at it in horror. Was it that bad? I haven't dared to look.

"This wouldn't happen to have anything to do with Mr. Michael would it?" he asked. I looked at him.

"You know about Michael?" I asked. "Do you both?"

"My dear, everyone knows about Michael." Arthur said as he led me to a table. It looked like an old examination table. I got onto the table and he started to move around the room, grabbing random things. I wasn't really paying attention to what they were. I took my shirt off knowing it would be better for hm to examine the wound better.

"Everyone knows? Do they know what he can do?" I asked. Arthur lightly pushed me down to lay on the table.

"Of course, everyone knows. They just don't do or say anything. Some of us tried to free him from his brother-" Arthur was saying, but I cut him off. I was completely shocked.

"That guy is Michael's brother?! Why doesn't their parents do anything to stop me?" I asked. Arthur and Jerry exchanged looks. "What? Am I missing something?"

"Their parents died eight year ago. There was an accident and they didn't make it." Jerry said.

"What happened?" I asked. I winced when Arthur applied pressure. He muttered a 'sorry' but continued to work. I looked over to Jerry, waiting for his answer.

"No one is really sure. Some say Derek did it so he can use his brother for his own personal gain. Others say Michael got angry and flung them across the room. He was a kid and couldn't control anything." Jerry said. "Shortly after they died Derek dropped out of school. He started to go by 'D' and started to do what he does now."

"First he had Michael steal money from banks and have Michael throw people around to show people how powerful he is." Arthur said. "And it worked. Soon people were scared he would have Michael do something terrible if they didn't do what Derek wanted them to do."

"Anyone know the truth about what really happened?" I asked.

"Michael and his brother. They were both there." Arthur said. "There was one other person, but people just thought he was crazy."

"What's his name?" I asked. I got up from the table when Arthur was finished. I flinched when I moved the wrong way as I put my shirt back on.

"Josh. Josh Turner." Arthur said. "But you can't see him. He is in what kids call the wacky shack. Derek put him there after the attack."

"Doesn't mean I can't try to go talk to him." I said. Arthur left the room for a moment and came back with some blankets.

"At least sleep here for the night." Arthur said. I took the blankets he offered and went to the couch, already planning to talk to Josh in the morning as sleep took over and my eyes closed.

I woke up the next morning to smell amazing coming from somewhere in the house. I slowly sat up, feeling the ache of everything that happened to me yesterday. On the table in front of me was a bottle of pain relievers and a glass of water. I smiled at the gesture. I put some in my mouth and drank all the water. I started to remember the conversation from last night with Arthur and Jerry. The same Josh Turner came to mind. I needed to talk to him, but I guess I'll have to go through some people first. If Michael's brother is the one that put him there then there is a chance, I'll be his first visitor in years, maybe his only visitor at all.

"I see you're awake," Jerry said, getting my attention from the doorway leading somewhere else in Arthur's house.

"Thank you for bringing me. I know helping me was risky, but I don't know where I'd be right now if you didn't bring me to Arthur to look at me." I said.

"You didn't seem like the type to give up and I believe that's what Michael needs." Jerry said, smiling at me. There was silence in the room as my stomach made a growling sound. "Hungry?" Jerry asked, chuckling as my face turned a shade of red.

"Last time I ate was before I came to town." I admitted.

"Well, let's get you some food." Jerry said. I followed him into the kitchen where there were plates on the kitchen table. Different kinds of eggs and toast were on different plates on the table along with plates of sausage and bacon. "Go ahead. Dig in." Jerry handed me a plate. Arthur came in as I started to pile food onto my plate. They both gave me weird looks as I ate. I just shrugged it off.

"Are you sure you don't want us to go with you?" Arthur asked as I finished. "It could be dangerous."

"Thanks for the offer, but no thanks. I think I need to speak to him alone." I said. They both nodded at me as I got up. I thanked them both and walked out of the house. I stood there in the street, looking from left to right. No one was on the street. I looked around one last time before walking down the street, making my way to where Jerry told me Josh was being kept. The building was tall and it looked like bars were on every window like this was a prison. I walked up to the entrance, passing people like I belonged entering the building.

"Can I help you ma'am?" the receptionist asked. Her nametag said her name is Kelly.

"Yes, you can actually. I'm here to see Josh Turner." I said. She looked at me like she was seeing two heads.

"Uh…" she coughed, trying to compose herself. "Only… o-only relatives can see patients."

"He's my cousin," I lied. I know she has no reason to believe me, but this needs to work. I need to get in. "Let me talk to my cousin," I said in a stern voice.

"He's on the third floor," she said before pressing a buzzer that made a loud sound and double doors on my left opened. I thanked her and walked through the doors. I know the second those doors close she'll be calling Derek so I better talk to him fast.

I walked by all the workers with their patients. None of the patients would look at me as I passed them and the workers didn't care enough to look. I came to a shut door. It's the only shut door I've seen. The name tag next to the door said Josh Turner. I turned the knob and slowly opened the door before walking through. The room looked like a bedroom and living room combined. There was a bed and a desk, but also a bookshelf filled with his back facing me. He looked like he could be young, maybe the same age as me, but I won't be able to tell until he turns around.

"I don't feel like playing chest today Chester, sorry," he said, not turning around.

"Well good thing my name is not Chester." I said. "And I don't know how to play chess." He turned around and looked at me. His gaze went up and down.

"Who are you?" he asked. "What do you want?"

"Well…" I said, walking over to his recliner and sitting down. "There is something we need to talk about."

"And what is it?" he asked, sitting on his bed facing me. "What is so important for us to talk about that you had to sneak your way in here? How did you even get in here?"

"I told them you're my cousin. Look I don't have a lot of time. They probably already told him I'm here so let's make this quick." I said. "I need to know what happened to Michael's parents."

"I don't know what you're talking about." Josh said, standing back up. He went back to the window. His back went back to me, but I knew he was shocked by what I said.

"Cut the crap. I know you do. Quicker you tell me, the quicker I can save him from his brothers." I said. He turned around and leaned against the window and lean.

"It was eight years ago," he started.

"That is Okay, just remember what you can." I said. He chuckled, but didn't say anything.

"Derek and I were seventeen and Michael was eight. Derek was my best friend and Michael worshipped him like most little brothers did."

"Continue." I said when he stopped talking and was staring at me from the window.

"We were hanging out at his house that day. I lived in a foster home with a lot of kids so we always hung out at his place. A huge storm was on its way so we agreed to stay at the house so that their mom wouldn't worry about us. Derek and I were playing video games in the living room and Michael was outside in the yard. The storm was coming closer and closer, so their mom had asked Michael to come in, but he didn't want to. Their mom asked Derek and I to get him inside. We went out to try, but he argued with us. Eventually we had to carry him in. Just as the storm hit, he started to throw a fit and something happened." Josh said, getting lost in his own words.

"What happened?" I asked, wanting him to continue.

"Things started to life off the ground and spin around. Everything from the furniture to the papers on the table. The more he screamed, the more things started to fly. Before we all know it everything in the downstairs rooms were all flying. We all tried to take cover. I ran to the stairs. Derek was trying to calm Michael down enough to make it all stop. Eventually he calmed down and everything fell to the ground with a loud thud." Josh said.

"What happened to their parents?" I asked. I had to admit this is not something I pictured happening.

"Their mom was found in the kitchen. She had three knife wounds in her chest. She was still alive when Derek found her, but she died in the hospital a few hours later. We found their dad a few yards away. It looked as though some things flew into him. His skull was crushed." Josh said.

"Was Michael accused?" I asked.

"No. Derek made up some story about us being attacked by some people who was trying to rob the house. He even made sure it was believable." Josh said, pulling his shirt up revealing some scars across his torso. I was about to ask him what Derek did to make those scars when someone came barging into the room. It was the receptionist that let me in, Kelly.

"You need to go," she said to me.

"You told him I was here." I guessed. She nodded and looked down.

"I'm sorry, but I had to. We were instructed to notify him if anyone visits Josh." Kelly said.

"Let me guess he is on his way." I said.

"No. We have orders to capture you and hand you over to him," she said. I looked at Josh.

"I know, but I'll be fine," he said. "You need to go. Now!" I nodded and left the room with Kelly. We walked down the hall towards the exit doors.

"FIND HER NOW!" I heard someone shout behind us. I pushed Kelly into the nearest supply closet.

"You're going to say I attacked you and pushed you in here. You got that?" I asked. She nodded at me. "I want you to have yourself and Josh ready by tonight and I will come for you."

"But I-" she started to say, but I cut her off.

"Just do it. I'll be back after I get Michael." I said. I went to turn around, but she grabbed me.

"Are you insane?" she asked. I got out of her grip then went to the door and walked out.

I checked to make sure the hall was clear before making my way to the exit doors. It was easy getting to the door, almost too easy. I touched the door when it hit me. Two things could happen. One, I could open the doors and an alarm could go off alerting the people who are trying to find me. Or two, I could go towards the voices I just hears and be captured that way. Either way I can't through the doors. I went back to Josh's room. He was still in there.

"What are you still doing here?" he asked, shocked to see me.

"I have to find a new exit." I said. I opened his window enough for me to go through. No one seemed to be outside. I just have to get through the bars. They seemed wide enough.

"Are you insane?" Josh asked, pulling me away from the window.

"Why does everyone ask me that?" I asked.

"You can't go out my window. It's three stories up." Josh said. "You'll break your neck."

"Do you have a better idea?" I asked. "If I go out the doors I won't make it out and I won't be able to help Michael or you."

"Well you can't just jump down," he said, going over to his bed. "You need something to help you get down." I watched ass he tied two of his sheets together. He looked at me. "I saw this in a movie once." He walked over to the window. He tied one end to the bars and threw the rest out of the window, making the sheets linger towards the grounds.

"What do I do now?" I asked, raising my eyebrow.

"Hoist yourself through the bars and over the edge holding onto the sheets." Josh said. "Put your feet against the building and walk down."

"What if I fall?" I asked, nervously looking down to the ground.

"Well, there's a ground to break your fall," he said. I looked at him before hoisting myself over the edge of the window and through the bars. I grabbed onto the sheets and then let myself dangle. I dangled there for a second before placing both feet on the building and walked myself down. I reached the ground and looked up. Josh was still in the window. I waved at him before I watched him being pulled in. I was about to run back in, but I stopped myself. I have to save Michael first. I started running away, but stopped when I realized something.

I don't know where Michael is.

If I was someone who was holding my own brother close to me or somewhere no one would look, where would it be? My eyes widened and I started to run, feeling the ache and pain from yesterday. I could hear the police sirens that were no doubt looking for me. Of course, he's got the police on his side. I took every alley until I reached the outside of town. I spotted the house I once saw Michael go into. The sirens were getting closer. This was my last chance. I ran toward the house. The front door was locked and all the windows were closed. There were some old chairs broken in the yard. I grabbed a broken piece and threw it into the window. The broken piece of the chair busted through the window and I climbed in, staying away from the broken glass.

"MICHAEL!" I called out into the empty house.

There was no answer.

"MICHAEL!" I called out again.

There was still no answer.

Maybe he wasn't here. Maybe he was in a different place, but then the sirens that seemed to be getting closer wouldn't be coming here. No, he's here. I just need to find him before people came here. I ran up the stairs and checked every room, but they were all empty. I went back downstairs and spotted a door with four locked on it. Now why would you need four locks on one door? I looked around for something hard to try to bang the locked open, but there was nothing there. I quickly went back through the window and found a huge rock. I carried it back into the house and started to bang on the locked until they all broke off. I opened the door and slowly walked down the steps and into a room. I found Michael in a ball in the corner. He looked badly beaten. He looked up at me and slightly smiled.

"I told you I would come for you."

CHAPTER 2

The Kid

"WE NEED TO move somewhere and hide." I said as I heard people outside all taking at once.

"I know a place." Michael said. He got up and walked over to the other side of the basement we were in. I walked over to see Michael opening something. "It's a small cupboard space. I used to hide here when I didn't want my brother to find me."

"So, he doesn't know that this is here?" I asked. Michael shook his head. A big noise was heard from above as people entered the house. Michael and I quietly climbed into the space. It was small and barely big enough to fit the both of us, but we still shut the door and sat in silence.

We listened as people walked all around the house. My breath hitched as I heard the stairs creak. By the sounds of how much the stairs creaked it was more than one person that was coming into the basement, at least five or more person coming down stairs.

"I told you she's here. If those broken locks weren't proof enough then how about the fact that Michael isn't down here like he should be?" Derek said. By the tone of his voice. I could tell he was beyond pissed.

"Well, she couldn't have gotten far," someone said. "We'll find her Derek."

"You better or something bad will start happening to people in this town." Derek said. I heard the stairs creak again as people went back upstairs. We stayed where we were until we heard all the cars drive away. Slowly, we both got out and made our way up the creaky stairs. I slowly looked out the door to make sure no one was in the room. Slowly, looking all around the room we made our way to the window. I came out and poked my head out of the window and made our way through the surrounding forest to Arthur's back door with the intent to have to help leaving Jamestown.

"Are we there yet?" Michael asked for the millionth time.

"No, we aren't there yet. I still don't know where we are going." I said. Michael groaned in annoyance and leaned back in his seat, closing his eyes. He reopened them a second later and looked at me.

"We have been in this car for days. Can we find a hotel or something? I refuse to spend another night in this car at some rest stop regardless if they have a bathroom or not." Michael said.

"You know what, you're right. We should get a hotel room. We both could use an actual bed to sleep on and a shower wouldn't hurt." I said, not liking being in the car either. I saw a hotel we were approaching and started towards it.

"Finally!" Michael said. He smiled widely as I pulled into the hotel. I parked and headed into the office, leaving Michael alone in the car. There was an old woman sitting behind the counter. She looked u[at me as I walked up to the counter. She smiled nicely at me as I placed my shaky hands on the counter. I tried to tell myself to stay calm.

"Can I help you miss?" she asked, sweetly.

"Yes. I would like a room please, one with two beds." I said.

"I believe we have a few rooms like that available," she said.

"Do you have any rooms close to the main office? I have my son who prefers to be near the office." I said.

"We do. Will you be paying in cash or credit?" she asked.

"Credit." I said. I pulled my wallet out and handed her a credit card. She typed up information into the computer and handed me back the card. I slipped it back into my wallet as she handed me two keys, both saying room 2.

I walked back out of the office and to the car which was now empty. I checked every seat in the car and no one was in any of the seats and nothing seemed broken.

"Michael?!" I shouted. There wasn't an answer. I started to panic. They couldn't have found him already. I don't even know where we are, so they couldn't have. "MICHAEL!"

"Yes?" Michael said from behind me. I whipped around in the direction of his voice to see him coming from a road that lead to a town we were close to.

"Don't do that!" I shouted at him.

"I just went to see if there was anything nearby. I didn't go that far." Michael said. I sighed.]

"If you're going to go anywhere even if it's a few feet away please tell me first." I said. "I know it doesn't seem like a big deal, but your brother or his goons could be anywhere."

"I did not think of that. I'm sorry." Michael said. I went over to the trunk of the car.

"You can shower first and then let's get some sleep." I said. Michael nodded and I opened the trunk of the car. Michael grabbed both bags and we headed to the room.

"Do you think Josh and Kelly are alright?" Michael asked.

"I'm sure they are fine." I said. Michael nodded and we walked into the room. Truth is, I didn't know if that was the correct answer. After I left out of Josh's window and he got pulled back in I didn't see him again. I wanted to look for them, but my main goal was to get Michael out of there. I promise I'd go back for them and one day I will. After Arthur gave me his car and I left with Michael I told Michael everything as we drove away.

An hour later, I was getting ready to take a shower. Michael was watching some horror movie he found on television so I took this time to lock the door and windows before going to the bathroom and locking myself in there. I had the water running, getting warm when I looked at myself in the mirror. There was bags under my eyes. We left Jamestown days ago and I haven't really slept since. I just couldn't sleep. Once the water was warm enough I undressed myself and stepped in. The water hit my muscles and I felt myself relax for the first time since I arrived in Jamestown. For a few moments I didn't worry about anything and my mind was clear. I cleaned myself up and stood in the water until the water turned cold. I shut the water off and climbed out, the cold air hitting my already cold skin making me shiver and quickly wrap myself in a towel. I got into clean clothes, put my damp hair into a messy bun, and left the bathroom. I heard snoring coming from Michael's bed telling me Michael fell asleep. I turned off whatever movie he was watching before I climbed into my bed and closed my eyes, letting the exhaustion take over.

I was woken by the sound of the theme song of some television show. I sat up quickly on the bed. Michael was at the end of the bed fully clothed in different clothes with a plate in his hands. I looked around the room. There was another plate with eggs, bacon, and toast on it. I looked back at Michael. He still hasn't noticed I was awake. I rolled my eyes and got out of bed, going straight to the plate waiting for me. Silence filled the room, only thing being heard was the show on the television playing and forks hitting plates as we ate. Watching Michael concentrate on the television show had me curious about something.

"Michael?" I asked. He didn't look at me. "Michael?!" I tried again only louder. I got his attention. I laughed and rolled my eyes. He looked at me and waited for me to say something. "Your brother, he didn't let you watch television or anything normal kids do did he?"

"Not really. Not after our parents died." He took a moment. "At first things were okay, great even. Derek was eighteen, so he was able to adopt me. He said he didn't want me be some kid that had to adapt to a new family. He wanted us to stay together. He was like my brother and dad at the same time. We did everything together. We went out to dinner and went ice skating. My favorite was rainy days. We would rent movies and buy loads of junk food and buy take out. Then we would make a giant fort in the living room and just spend the day watching the movies and eating all the food until our stomachs hurt. It was just us two and the world outside didn't matter. Only us mattered." Michael smiled slightly. "It was like all the bad things that happened didn't matter."

"When did it all change?" I asked. I walked over and sat with him. He leaned on me and out his head on my shoulder. I smiled at the gesture and wrapped an arm around him.

"About nine months after the accident. I was still seven, turning eight in a few weeks. I haven't really used the power since that day.

Derek started to make me practice my power." Michael said. "He turned our childhood home into a practice range. He'd make me pick things up and throw them around like I did the way of the accident." There has to be something to get his mind off things.

"Hey Michael, have you ever been to a mall before?" I asked.

The mall wasn't that far from the hotel. Just ten miles down the road. Three minutes after the intense conversation with Michael, we were getting into the car. Michael was not holding in his excitement as I drove. The drive went quick, Michael bouncing in his seat the entire time. He bounced even more the second the sign to the mall came into view. I laughed as I parked the car and he hurried out before I could turn off the ignition. I got out and walked behind Michael. My eyes looking everywhere. I couldn't help it. Being out in the open was risky.

"Michael, wait for me here." I said when we walked in. Michael nodded and sat at a bench nearby. I walked into the ladies' room. I was in there for almost ten minutes before I walked back out of the ladies' room expecting Michael to be sitting there on the bench, but unfortunately he wasn't. I started walking around the mall, hoping he went into a random store. I looked through every store window I went by. I was about to get to the end of the mall when I saw Michael. I was relieved, but the relief went away when I watched him get pulled back. "MICHAEL!" I shouted, making everyone around me turn their heads and give me a weird look. I started to fast walk, turning it into a run to get to where I saw Michael get pulled back. My mind was racing with thoughts that his brother caught us already. I finally got there and turned the corner. A kid who looked not that much older than Michael maybe even the same age was holding Michael to the wall. He was saying something to Michael. It was low and I couldn't hear or make it out so I got closer.

"If you think about running away, I will still find you." I heard the kid say as I got closer.

"Hey!" I shouted. "Back off my son!"

'Back off lady," the kid said, pushing me. I landed on the ground with a loud thud. I looked up to see the anger in Michael's eyes, just like in the hotel lobby. He looked around before looking at the kid. The kid took a step towards me. I could tell he was going to do something so I closed my eyes waiting for an impact. Nothing happened. I heard a shout and opened eyes to see the kid in the air, heading towards the ceiling. I quickly looked around to see no one paying attention. I looked back at Michael and then the kid in the air. The kid looked terrified. It reminded me of when I first saw Michael use his power in the alley.

"Leave her alone!" Michel said in a stern voice that even gave me the chills. Michael let him go. The kid dropped to the ground. He took off running. Michael walked over and held his hands out to me. "Are you okay?" He helped me up.

"Yes." I said, brushing off my pants. "What happened?" I asked.

"I got bored so I went to the nearest store and was looking through the window when he came up to me and stood next to me." Michael said.

"Did he say anything?" I asked.

"At first he didn't say anything." Michael said. "He followed me as I walked to each window. I tried not to go far. After a few windows, that is when he spoke."

"What did he say?" I asked.

"He said he knew my secret. He said he knew about my power. He threatened to expose me if I didn't follow him." Michael said. "So, I followed."

"Do you use your power at the mall?" I asked. "Did someone see you?"

"No. I don't know how he knew. I never saw him before." Michael said. "What are we going to do about it?"

"We'll have to find him."

Three days. I have been looking for this kid for three days. He was nowhere to be found. It was like he just vanished into thin air after Michael dropped him on the mall floor. I moved Michael and I to a different hotel, one that was better and had more stuff for Michael to do. I haven't let him leave the hotel since it happened. I knew from the look on his face when Michael used his power that the kid didn't know what the power was, but then how did he know Michael had a power in the first place?

"I'm going to go try to find him again." I said as I grabbed the car keys and my bag. Michael looked at me from the couch he was laying on. He was spaced out on the couch watching something on the television. It looked like another horror movie.

"Why? You've been looking for three days. It's a lost cause." Michael said. "He's gone by now and hopefully for good."

"I can't give up. He knows what you can do. Who knows what could happen now?" I said. "Your brother could find out about the kid. He could find him and find out where we are."

"Alright. I get it." Michael said, putting his hands up. "Bring back some pizza when you're done please. I'm over room service."

The hallway smelt like peperoni pizza as I stepped off the elevator with Michael's pizza in my hands. I can't believe I struck out again. Today is Monday so I went to the high school around the time kids get out of school and blended in with the parents who were waiting for their kids. The bell rang and kids came out. My eyes were going to every face I could see, but he never came out. I hit the steering wheel in frustration, making the horn go off and everyone turn their heads in my direction. I quickly left the high school and went to get Michael's pizza and went back to the hotel. If I showed up at the hotel without the pizza Michael would not be pleased and I would never head the end of it. I got to the hotel room and quickly opened the door, not wanting to hold the pizza anymore.

"Hey Michael, I got you your-" I stopped when I walked in. I was frozen in place. Michael was sitting on the couch laughing with the kid. "What's going on?"

"Oh hey. You're back!" Michael said as I just stared at them. I was still frozen. I've been searching for days and he just randomly shows up. How does he even know where we are?

"I knew where you were because I sensed him," the kid said. How did he even know what I was wondering? I didn't say anything. "You know you were thinking out loud, right?" he asked, laughing. "Oh and the name is Anthony, but you can call me Tony. Everyone does."

"What do you mean you sensed him?" I asked, finally moving and setting the pizza down. "I've been searching for you. Where have you been?"

"Out of town." Tony said. "I left because I thought you were going to hunt me down."

"Do I look like the hunting type to you?" I asked. He laughed and shook his head, answering no.

"I know you want answers so let's make a deal. You share the pizza and I'll answer your questions." Tony said.

"Deal." I said. Tony smiled. I served the boys pizza before getting my own and sitting down. I nibbled on the pizza while Tony tried to explain to Michael what video games are. Tony couldn't believe how little Michael knows.

Three hours later, the pizza was gone, the sundaes I ordered were finished and everyone was relaxing. Michael, looking bored, was flipping through channels on the television.

"So, you wanted to know things?" Tony asked. I looked at him, but he wasn't looking at me. He was looking at Michael.

"I do, yes." I said. He turned and looked at me. "Where did you go? And don't say anything about hunting you. You know we weren't. I was just trying to find you to talk to you. I wasn't going to hurt you."

"True. I knew you weren't." Tony said. "Truth is after Mikey did what he did I got freaked out and I took off out of town."

"Where did you go? I looked for you for three days. It was like you disappeared." I said.

"I didn't disappear. I just went a couple cities over to see my mom." Tony said.

"Is that where you really live? With her a couple cities over?" I asked.

"No. She's... she is..." Tony started to say, but he couldn't get the words out. He seemed to be really struggling. Michael looked at us, finally paying attention. "She's in..."

"She's in a wacky shack." Michael said, smirking. Tony sighed.

"She's not in a wacky shack." Tony said, folding his arms defensively. "She is in a rehabilitation clinic."

"So, she's in a wacky shack?" Michael asked, smirking. Tony sighed.

"Why does everyone have to be there? First Josh and now your mom. What is wrong with people?" I said mainly to myself.

"Who's Josh?" Tony asked, but I ignored him and Michael answered.

"A guy who used to be my brother's best friend. He was put there days after my power started." Michael explained. "My power crazed brother locked him up so he couldn't say anything to anyone."

"We need a plan to get your mom out." I said, walking back and forth.

"What?" Tony asked, but I ignored him again.

"We need a plan. I mean we can't just walk in there. Been there, done that." I said. "Doesn't always work, but we can use it as a backup plan."

"WAIT! HOLD ON!" Tony shouted, finally getting my attention. He was standing neat the window now. He was looking out it like something was bothering him.

"We can get her out." Michael said. "All we need is a plan. She is great with a plan, I think."

"Don't you two get it?" Tony asked, facing us. "I don't want you to get her out. She belongs there."

"What do you mean she belongs there?" I asked.

"She is better off there." Tony said.

"She can't be better off there." I said. "No one belongs in a place like that."

"She's been there since I was five." Tony said, sitting back down on the couch. "I had just turned five when my sister Anna disappeared, someone took her from our lawn. I mean who kidnaps a twelve-year-old from a lawn in a gated community? My mom slowly went nuts trying to find her. No one was really helping to look for her. She was the first to disappear in the community so no one really knew what to think or do."

"Did anyone find her?" I asked.

"No. She's been missing for over ten years." Tony said.

"So... your mom..." I said.

"She went nuts trying to find her and when they couldn't be had a funeral even though she wasn't in there and it got worse after that. She started talking to herself more and more. She even said she was taking to Anna. She started to stop eating slowly. At first it started off missing a mean here or there, but then she started skipping a meal a day and then more and more meals until she stopped eating completely. She started forgetting I was even there. I had to learn to take care of myself and make my own meals or else I wouldn't have survived. She got lost in her old little world and she had to be committed for it and she's been there ever since." Tony said.

"I'm sorry," I said as I sat next to him.

"It was twelve years ago. Sure, sometimes I picture what my life would be like if no one took my sister. She would still be alive and I'd still have my mom." Tony said.

"Wait, if your mom went all wacky shack where did you go?" Michael asked.

"No one knew where my dad was so my mom's sister took me in. It was me and her three boys. They didn't like that I was there. I mean my aunt loves me and all, but I always felt like her charity case. I ran away two years ago." Tony said. "I've been on my own since. I'm doing good if I say so myself."

"When was the last time you ate before the pizza and sundaes or took a shower or even had a decent place to sleep?" I asked. He said nothing. He just shrugged his shoulders.

"Well now you can be stuck with us." Michael said. I nodded in agreement. Tony smiled.

The next morning, I woke up to hearing voices. Not like the in my head kind of voices, but the voices of Michael and Tony. They were trying to whisper, but they weren't doing a very good job since I could hear every word they were saying.

"I can't do that to her." I heard Michael say. "She protects me. She's done more for me than anyone has in the past eight years. You don't understand how bad my brother is. I can't just leave."

"I'm not saying doing this forever. Just for a few hours." Tony said. "When's the last time you did anything fun?"

"I don't know, but sneaking out? Do you really think that's a good idea?" Michael asked. "Can't we just tell her where we're going?"

"We'll leave a note Mikey." Tony said. "We'll only be gone a couple of hours. We'll have some fun and be back for dinner."

This is when I decided to show I'm awake. I moved my legs and sat up. The boys immediately went quiet and looked at me. I stayed quiet and got up. I didn't want them to know I was listening. I got myself a cup of coffee and sat with the boys at the table. Tony put a plate of eggs, toast, and bacon in front of me. I started to eat as I eyes the boys who were eyeing each other. I slightly laughed. I thought about what I heard Tony say. Michael has gone through a lot and with the way his brother was I doubt Michael has been a kid in a long time. Maybe they could go out together. I could use a day alone and I don't see what could go wrong especially when no one knows where we are. Heck, I don't even know where we are. They were still eyeing each other without trying to look at each other. Maybe I should bring up the subject to them before their eyes pop out of their heads.

"Do you think you two can handle a day without me?" I asked. They looked at each other before looking at me. They slowly nodded their heads like they were unsure. "Good. I would like to do some things that don't require the company of two teenage boys. You two can go have some fun around town if you'd like. I can leave some money before I go."

"Y-yeah... yeah that sounds great." Tony said. I got up, putting my plate with theirs before setting a credit card on the table and heading into the bathroom to get ready for my day alone without the boys. I could hear them whispering to each other that they couldn't believe what just happened as I walked into the bathroom and closed the door, locking it behind me.

Eight hours later and I was walking back into the hotel room and closed the door. I felt a lot better. I spend the day at the hotel spa being pampered. I even got a haircut and made my hair shorter thinking Derek wouldn't be able to recognize me if he saw me with shorter hair. Now I am refreshed the boys should be back any minute. I decided to take them out to dinner instead of just ordering something from room service. I jumped slightly when I heard something slam against the door. I quickly went to the door and opened it, only to have Tony fall to the ground in front of me bloody and bruised.

"TONY!" I shouted. I helped him up and onto the couch. I ran to the first aid kit Arthur gave me before leaving Jamestown and was storing in my bag. I hurried back to Tony. "What happened?"

"We took the card you left us." Tony started to say. He winced as I touched the cut above his eye. "We went to the movies since Mikey said he never actually been to the movies."

"You only went to see a movie?" I asked, cleaning more cuts.

"Not just that then we went to get a bite to eat, but everything was still fine. We got some burgers. After that Mikey started to get nervous. He kept saying someone was following us, but I just thought he was being paranoid since I didn't see anyone." Tony said. "We were about to enter an arcade when people jumped us. At first, I thought they were thugs or something because they were huge guys, but then this guy walked over to Mikey and said something to him in his ear. He looked from me to him before Mikey agreed to go with him."

"Who took him? Do you know?" I asked. Tony nodded his head before telling me the three words I dreaded the most.

"His brother, Derek."

CHAPTER 3

Back to Jamestown

I REALIZED TONY'S INJURIES were only minor after I cleaned his wounds. There weren't any broken bones. Just a few cuts on his face and bruises all over his back, chest, and arms. Tony was now sleeping peacefully on the couch so I pulled my phone out and dialed a number I was given when I left Jamestown.

"Hello?" a voice answered after a fifth ring.

"Arthur? It's Nicole." I said into the phone.

"Nicole… as in…" he started to say but got lost for words.

"The woman who saved Michael." I finished for him. "I don't have much time. I am calling because something bad has come up."

"What is it?" he asked. "Are you all safe?"

"We have a problem." I said. "I'm miles from Jamestown. Probably states even and I had Michael we were safe."

"Had? Were? What do you mean?" Arthur asked.

"Well… he found us or at least the people that work for him did." I said. "He took Michael back."

"What do you mean he took Michael back? He shouldn't have been able to find you." Arthur said. "I put new license plates on the car. He shouldn't have been able to find you unless you did something stupid and used your actual credit cards and he tracked those down, but you were smart enough to use cash for everything, right?"

"Um…" I said, slightly shifting my weight not that he could see. I know I was doing something wrong this whole time. Why didn't I think of that?

"Nicole are you serious?!" Arthur asked very loudly. "You used your real credit card?!"

"I know, I know. I screwed up. I feel bad enough." I said.

"You go on the run, you use cash for everything so you can't be traced. Didn't movies or television shows teach you anything?" Arthur asked.

"I'm sorry. I screwed up." I said. "Just keep an eye on things until I get there. I'm on my way." I hung up the phone, tossing it on the bed. I sighed loudly in frustration.

The next morning, I packed mine and Michael's things and put them in the car. Tony was still sore from yesterday as he slowly got into the car. I got into the car and started it. Neither of us has said a word all morning. Our true destination was Jamestown, but I knew we needed to make a quick stop in the opposite direction before heading to Jamestown.

"Where are we going?" Tony asked when I started driving. "Isn't Jamestown the other way?"

"Yes. We aren't going to Jamestown yet." I said. "We are making a stop for you to see your mom first."

"Why are you taking me to see my mom?" Josh asked. "We need to get to Jamestown."

"We will." I said. "You need to see your mom before we go."

"Why?" Tony asked. "Why do you care so much about me, about my mom, about Michael, or our powers? What makes you care?"

"I just do." I said.

"Why?" Josh asked again.

"A story for another time." I said.

The rest of the ride was silent. Tony was lost in his thoughts as I tried not to think of the real reason I started all of this. An hour later I parked in the parking lot of Saint Louis Home of the Mental Insane.

Tony got out without another word and went inside. Michael was already back in Jamestown under Derek's control. Tony came back twenty minutes later wiping his cheeks. I put my hand on his shoulder, not saying anything. I took my hand off his shoulder and started the car again. Tony looked back at the building as I drove out of the parking lot, heading in the direction of Jamestown. I could tell him things will be alright and he will see his mom again, but the truth was I don't know if that could happen. I don't know what is going to happen. All I do know is that I won't be letting anyone else get hurt.

It took eight days to drive back to Jamestown with the stops we made. Stops for gas and snacks for the road. The stops at random restaurants when we were hungry. Spending two hours in awkward silence with strangers around us as we ate. No one really talked other than to order drinks and food. Stopping at hotels when it became too dark to see the road and the air in the car was too thick to keep moving. It was like someone was all the oxygen out of the car the more we drove. I knew that Tony was blaming himself for Michael's abduction, but it was not his fault. I was also blaming myself, but at least I know it is.

I pulled up to Arthur's house. Jerry was sitting on the steps probably waiting for us. Before I could even turn the car off and get out of the car Jerry was squeezing himself into the back seat. I didn't have time to question things. He grabbed my phone and typed something into the GPS. Silence filled the car as I followed the directions the phone gave me. I kept eyeing Jerry in the rearview mirror, but he never looked my way, only out the window. I pulled up to an old house. It looked like it was built in the late nineties. It looked beautiful. Jerry got out of the car and walked into the house.

"Should we follow?" Tony asked, looking at the house.

"I think so, but first I need to say something." I said, turning the car off and facing Tony. "Michael being taken I know you blame yourself, but it's not your fault. It's mine actually."

"How is it yours?" Tony asked.

"I'm new to the whole on the run thing so I didn't think about not using my own credit cards and I used my own credit cards at the hotels and they tracked us down to where we were." I said. Tony rolled his eyes and got out of the car. I sighed and got out of the car as well. I looked around. There was a garden off to the side blocked off by a fence so no one touched it. I walked into the house and into a long hallway expecting Arthur to be here, but he wasn't. "Where's Arthur?"

"Sit down." Jerry said. I walked into the living room and sat down on a couch. Jerry handed me a drink. I took a sip and then coughed loudly. Vodka.

"Kind of strong." I said.

"Well you're going to need it for this." Jerry said. I stared at him for a few minutes as I waited for him to answer. "You texted Arthur's phone when you let him know you were just a few miles out and he responded saying that he couldn't wait to see you."

"How do you know that?" I asked. "Did Arthur tell you?"

"No. It wasn't Arthur that answered you." Jerry said. I looked from Jerry to Tony and then back to Jerry.

"Wait, if he didn't answer me then who did?" I asked. I am so confused by where this is going.

"The night you called to tell us Michael had been taken again by his brother Arthur suffered a heart attack." Jerry said.

"I made him have a heart attack." I said.

"No, you didn't." Jerry said. "He always had heart problems. He was fine after it happened. They kept him overnight for observation and they had planned on releasing him the next day depending on how he did during the night. I left when visitation hours were over and he was fine, but by the time I returned the next morning he had mysteriously stopped breathing." He gave me that look that made me realize what really happened.

Someone helped him stop breathing.

"Where did you burry him?" I asked. Jerry handed me a piece of paper from his pocket like he knew I was going to ask with a plot number on it. I left without another word.

I drove through town, guilt eating me. I know what he meant when he said Arthur mysteriously stopped breathing. Something happened and it wasn't mysterious. I parked the car in an empty lot. I took a deep breath before stepping out of the car. This was the last thin I wanted to happen. I walked in the direction of his plot. I spotted his name Arthur McCulley beloved brother, husband, and friend. Next to his was AnneMarie McCulley beloved wife. The date on her grave was dated that she died twenty years ago. I bent down to his grave.

"I'm sorry," I began. "I'm sorry I brought you into this mess. I didn't know any of this would happen. It's my fault that they killed you. They took your life because I took Michael. Your death will always be on my hands. Who will be next? Jerry? Michael? Tony? You didn't even get to meet Tony. I was looking forward to that. He can make Michael really laugh. It was good to watch. I should have given up and left when I was told to.

"I agree. You should have given up," a voice said behind me. I turned around quickly and looked shocked. It was Derek, Michael's brother. I recognize him from the night at the bar.

"Derek." I said. He looked at me as if I was something he wanted to hurt. He probably did.

"D." he corrected me.

"Derek." I repeated. "What do you want?"

"Stay away from him." Derek said in a stern demanding voice.

"Stay away from who?" I asked.

"Stay away from Michael." Derek said. "He doesn't need you."

"Yeah because he needs you?" I asked. "Unlike you I don't plan on using him." He laughed, tilting his head back as he laughed.

"Why do you even care?" Derek asked. "Besides you will never find him so don't waste your time." He walked away.

Challenge accepted.

I got back to the house Jerry took us to. All the lights were off and everything was quiet. I didn't feel like going inside yet so I sat on the porch and looked around. It looked peaceful and beautiful here. I wondered if this was Jerry's house or something Arthur owned. I heard the door behind me open, but I didn't bother to get up or look behind me to see who it was.

"You alright?" Tony asked as he sat next to me.

"Where's Jerry?" I asked, ignoring his question.

"He went to bed. He said to pick a room." Tony answered. "Are you alright?" Tony asked again. I sighed.

"He was killed because of me. All because I tried to save someone." I said.

"You did save someone." Tony said. I looked at him.

"He was taken back." I pointed out to Tony.

"And we're going to get him back." Tony said. "I know that losing your friend is hard, but don't give up on Michael after one bump in the road."

"One bump in the road?" I asked. "Michael never told you what I had to do to save him did he?"

"We never really talked about it. I just know his brother is bad news." Tony said. I sighed.

"What if I get someone else killed?" I asked. "Like you, or Jerry, or Michael."

"You don't know if that could happen. I know your friend's death was tragic, but you can't let it stop you from saving Michael from his brother. He would not like that." Tony said.

"I guess you're right." I said, sighing.

"Of course I am." Tony said, making me laugh. "Now we should sleep. Jerry and I came up with a plan while you were gone."

And now I'm worried. This can't be a good thing.

"This is insane! This plan is insane! You both are on a suicide mission." I said after hearing their plan the next morning on the way to breakfast.

"It's not a suicide mission. It's a great plan." Tony said, defending their plan. "Jerry will call Michael's brother and tell him something false about you doing something to help Mikey and then we'll make our move."

"And what do you think will happen when he sends his goons and they discover the tip was fake?" I asked. "He could come after us or do something horrible to Michael or us."

"We... did not think of that." Jerry said.

"Let me tell you it won't be good." I said. "Thanks for trying, but they will tell him it was fake and nothing was there then he will find you and hurt you or worse kill you."

"Defiantly did not think of that." Tony said.

"We'll think of something else." Jerry said.

"Please do and one that doesn't get us killed." I said. "I'm hungry. Let's eat."

No one said anything. Forks hit plates. Drinks were being drank. Food went into mouths. You could literally hear the food being chewed. I have no idea what Tony and Jerry are thinking about, but my mind was on Michael. I couldn't help but wonder what he's doing or if he's alright.

If he was beaten up or if they left him alone. Has he eaten anything or if they were starving him? If something happened to him at all. He is all I can think about. I don't know about these two, but I care about Michael even though I just met him.

"We care about him too," Jerry said. I looked up from my plate with a raised eyebrow. "You were thinking out loud. It was like you were saying your own commentary."

"Oh, I didn't realize I was doing that." I said, completely embarrassed.

"She does that a lot." Tony commented.

"We do care. Everyone cares, but there is a difference between you and everyone else." Jerry said. I waited for him to tell me what difference that was, but he didn't speak. He just looked at me.

"And what difference is that?" I asked after he didn't say anything.

"You never gave up." Jerry said, putting another spoonful of food into his mouth.

"What are you talking about?" I asked. I waited until Jerry swallowed his food.

"We all tried to help him, everyone in town did. Most of us remember what Derek was like before their parents died and what he was like before he changed. We wanted to help Michael, but everyone tried and failed. Eventually we let Michal get abused and used by his brother. I sadly was included."

"But I didn't." I pointed out.

"No, you didn't." Jerry said, smiling proudly at me. "You kept trying to save him and yes his brother has him back, but I know you will save him again."

"You think so?" I asked, smiling to myself at Jerry's words.

"We both do." Tony said. The rest of the breakfast was silent as I thought of a plan to save Michael, a plan that could work and not get us injured or killed.

The plan seemed simple. I have been observing Derek for a few days. He had what seemed to be a small routine. He spent the morning where I thought he would in his childhood home and his afternoons in a small café having what he calls meetings with people he calls 'clients' which are really just people coming to him needing money and come back to the house at night, always bringing some sort of food with him. It left the house unoccupied for a few hours.

"Are you sure he is keeping Mikey in that house?" Tony asked as I got ready to leave Jerry's house.

"Well, that is their childhood home. It's where I found him last time and it's where Derek keeps returning to." I said. "There is no way to find out if he's in there."

"An old friend that owes me a favor is keeping Derek occupied for a little while longer." Jerry said. "I'll go do my part." Jerry left the house.

I looked at Tony. "Let's go."

"What? Me? Why? Me? No." Jerry nervously said as he followed me out. "I don't want to go."

"You can sense his power. That's how we will know if he is in the house or not." I said.

"Oh… yeah… I can totally do that." Tony said. I rolled my eyes and dragged him to the car. We got into the car and I started to drive towards the house. By now Derek should have left the house, but to be on the safe side I will be parking far away. Tony protested the whole way there and as I got out of the car, but I still made him get out. We moved among the trees that were surrounding the house, trying to stay out of sight since there was a few lights still on. I didn't see Derek or his goons outside anywhere so I'm guessing someone was inside where Michael could be.

"Is he in there?" I asked in a low voice. Tony wasn't paying attention so I smacked back of his head.

"Ow! What did you do that for?!" Tony shouted. I quickly covered his mouth.

"Shh! Are you insane?!" I whispered as the light inside was quickly turned off and someone came running out of the house. I ducked down and pulled Tony down with me, hard.

"What did I do?" Tony asked. I glared at him pointed to the goon now on the porch looking for any signs of us. "Oh."

"Quit talking!" I whispered. I slightly got back up. More goons were outside. There was one in the porch and the others were on the ground looking for us.

"Quick. Check the permeator!" the one of the porch shouted at the ones on the ground. "D said she'll show up eventually. Tonight must be our night." They all nodded and began to walk to the edge of the grounds, but they started walking on the other side completely opposite from we were.

"Do you feel him?" I asked Tony as I continued to watch them. Tony was watching them too. I had to nudge him to get his attention.

"Yeah I do. It's kind of weak compared to the last time I saw him, but I can feel him." Tony said. "That sounded dirty." Tony joked. I rolled my eyes.

"We've got one shot at this while their backs are turned." I said. He nodded at me.

Slowly, trying not to make any noise Tony and I made our way to the side of the house the goons weren't on. Going through the front door would be completely obvious since the first goon is still on the porch so I looked for a side door or an open window. There wasn't a side door, but close to the ground there was a broken window. The room looked dark, maybe the basement. I looked around to make sure none of the goons were looking. Luckily, they weren't. They were too busy looking in the forest to be paying attention. I looked around again and found the nearest stick. I hit the rest of the broken glass, making it easier for us to go through, but unfortunately the noise of the glass breaking was heard by the goons.

"Did you hear that?" someone asked.

"OVER THERE!" I heard a lot of them shout.

"They are coming." Tony said.

"We have to do something to get their attention away from us and the window." I said.

"I have an idea." Tony said.

"Wait-" I started to say, but Tony cut me off. He picked up a rock and threw it at the face of the first goon that was near us. "TONY!"

"COME AT ME BITCHES!" Tony shouted, running away from me. I jumped into the nearest shadow as every single goons ran after Tony. They chased Tony into the forest surrounding the house. I waited until I knew they were gone before stepping out of the shadow and into the house through the broken window. I grabbed the flashlight out of the backpack I had with me and turned it on.

I am definitely in the basement. I could see the whole in the wall Michael and I were in the last time I was in here, but the smell was toxic. The floor looked like it was covered in water and mold. Something must have burst from the last time I was in here. I gagged as I walked through the smelly mold t the creaky stairs. It smelled like a porter potty at the end of a festival. The stairs creaked as I walked up. It sounded like one of those old houses that have been so vacant people think they are haunted. I walked through the door and into the house. It looked like I was in the kitchen. I should have paid attention the last time I was in here. Being the way the outside of the house looked I pictured the inside looking the same and everything looking broken with trash everywhere, but the kitchen looked clean and everything I could see through the light from the flashlight was in its place. I wasn't kicking anything on the floor on my way to find Michael and when I shined the light into the sink the dishes were soaking in soapy water. I looked around with the flashlight, finding another doorway leading to somewhere else in the house. I went through the doorway, coming into a hallway. I felt the wall as I shined the flashlight around. I came across what felt like a photo frame. I pointed the flashlight at the photo frame. It was a photo of a family with two boys. The boys were young and smiling. Must have been Derek and Michael when they were younger. I heard a noise from somewhere in the house, making me jump and drop the photo. Was it a goon? I didn't hear any of them come in. I turned and pointed the flashlight in the direction the noise came from. Hunched over, someone was leaning against the wall.

"Michael?" I asked, walking towards the hunched person. The person looked up. It wasn't Michael, but they didn't look any better. I noticed who it really was. "Josh?"

"Hey," he said slowly. I went over and helped him up. "Back for the kid?"

"What happened to you?" I asked.

"They wanted information on where you were taking him. They have their ways to try to get information even if you don't actually have the information they want." Josh said. "And when the kid came back they needed a celebratory punching bag."

"I'm so sorry." I said, trying to hold Josh up while keeping a grip on the flashlight. Josh looked from me to the flashlight and then burst into laughter.

"Why are you using a flashlight? You do know the electricity works in here right?" Josh asked. "Everything works here. They turned the lights out when they heard something outside which I'm guessing was you. Derek keeps the outside like that so no one will bother coming around here looking for anything."

"What do you mean there's light?" I asked. Josh took the flashlight and shined the light on the wall. I noticed the light switch and walked over to flip the switch. The lights above shinned bright as the room lit up. It looked like a normal living room which shocked me. There was a couch, two love seats, a giant television, and a coffee table. To my left I could see stairs.

"He's up there in one of the rooms. I'll wait here and keep a lookout." Josh said. I nodded and made my way up the stairs.

I got to the top of the stairs. Five doors were closed I knew one of them was the bathroom so that left me with four options. I walked to the first door and opened it slowly. There was a normal bed with sleeping bags on the floor. Must be Derek's room. I went to the next door and opened it. I could immediately tell it was their parents room by the style, but why would they preserve the bedroom after all these years? I walked more into the room. The left side of the room held a photo of the two boys and a woman. This must be their mom's side of the room. I sat on the bed. There was a night stand with two drawers. Normally I wouldn't snoop, but I need to know if there is a way to beat Derek and maybe the mother had a solution I could use. There was only one way I could find out. The top drawer was filled with papers. I started pulling some out. First it was Derek's birth certificate. Then I pulled out a birth certificate for someone named Ryder dated two and a half years after Derek's, but I also found a death certificate for the same Ryder dated a year after the birth certificate. Digging more into the drawer I found adoption papers. Who was adopted?

"I was," someone said from behind me. I quickly turned around to see Michael standing in the doorway. "You were speaking aloud. Do you realize you do that a lot?"

"MICHAEL!" I shouted, jumping up. He quickly put his hand over my mouth.

"Do you want to get yourself caught?" Michael asked, rolling my eyes.

"You know about these?" I asked, ignoring his question and holding the papers up.

"I didn't until a few years ago. Derek never let me come in here, but I snuck in here one night after they brought me back and I found them." Michael said.

"Your name used to be Fernice?" I asked, looking at the papers and trying not to laugh.

"Don't laugh! According to those papers my parents were Amish and died in a car accident." Michael said. "I couldn't sleep when I came back and Derek went out celebrating my return with his so-called friends when I made sure he was gone I slipped in here. I don't know why he wants to keep the room like they are going to walk through the door any minute. Anyway, I started going through the drawer and I found all the papers."

"Who is Ryder?" I asked.

"Derek's younger brother and technically my older brother." Michael said. "He died when he was one. Derek and Ryder were taking a bath together and somehow Ryder ended up drowning."

"Apparently he was like this even back then." I said. "Did you ever ask your brother about these papers?" We somehow managed to move to the bed in the position of sitting Indian style across from each other with all the papers between us.

"I did. He pounded me for going into their room." Michael said. "It was the first time anyone out a hand on me since they found us and brought me back. After a while he sat me down and told me everything he knew."

"Did he know anything about your birth parents?" I asked. "Maybe you got your power from them."

"No. I even went through all my mom's diaries that I found, but there was no mention of them. And I don't want to know anything about them either. I killed my parents, the only parents I ever knew, the only ones I want to know."

"If it counts I think your mom would-" I was interrupted by Tony slamming into the room with Josh right behind him holding himself up.

"We have to get out of here. Now!" Tony said. "I was having them chase me and I was hiding from them when I overheard one of them calling Mikey's brother telling him you're here. He is on his way back now."

"Let's go now." I said. I turned to Michael. "Michael, if there's anything you want to take get it now. Hopefully you aren't coming back."

"Tony come help." Michael said. Tony nodded and they ran out. I took my phone out and dialed Jerry's number.

"Hello?" Jerry answered.

"Jerry, did you do what you were supposed to do?" I asked.

"Already done. I'm heading your way now." Jerry said.

"Drive faster. We have to get out of here now." I said.

"Got it. Be careful." Jerry said and I hung up.

Josh went down to be a lookout. I went back to look for Michael and Tony. I opened the next closed door, but I wish I hadn't. Laying on the floor was the receptionist that helped me leave. The smell coming from the room told me there was no point in checking for a pulse. I quickly shut the door and backed away. I stood there in shock for a moment before shaking my head and proceeding to find Michael and Tony. I found them in the last bedroom. Tony was holding a backpack and Michael was throwing random things into it. On the floor at Tony's feet was a garbage bag. I'm guessing that had his clothes in it. Michael finished throwing things into the backpack. Tony zipped it up and we left the room. Michael stopped in his parent's bedroom and came back out with a photo frame in his hands. He put it into the backpack and put the backpack on his back. We continued to leave. Josh was waiting at the bottom of the stairs. I could hear voices right outside. We quickly made our way down to the basement and to the window I came through. I peeked out the window to see all the goons surrounding the yard, more must have come and they were all waiting for us to leave the house.

"Can you run?" I asked Josh.

"I think so." Josh said. "You got a plan?"

"I think so." I said. "You and Tony will run in different directions and then meet up. Then meet up with us."

"What are you going to do?" Josh asked.

"I am going to get Michael past his brother." I said.

"How do you plan to do that?" Josh asked. "They all carry guns."

"I will figure that out. You two need to go before he gets here." I said.

"Where are we meeting?" Tony asked.

"You will need to find a white van in the woods surrounding the house. Jerry will be in it. He's waiting." I said. They nodded and climbed out the window. Tony first and then he helped Josh out. I peeked out and watched as Tony nodded to Josh before stepping forward.

"I'M BACK BITCHES!" Tony shouted. I ducked down and watched as everyone looked their way before some started running left after

Tony who kept yelling something back at them and some ran to the right as they went after Josh who was limping a bit as he ran. I waited until the yard was clean before standing up.

"Michael let's go." I said. I looked outside again before climbing out of the window. I turned around and grabbed Michael's bags and waited for him to climb out. We started crossing the yard. We were halfway across the yard to the forest when there was loud clapping heard from behind us.

"Bravo," Derek's voice was heard from behind us. We turned around and he was leaning against a car. One by one his goons came out from behind the trees and stood behind him like they needed an intense looking entrance.

"Derek." Michael said, pushing me behind him.

"Hello little brother." Derek said, getting off the car. He walked towards us. Every step he took towards us Michael took a step, making me back with him. "Oh come on Michael. Do you really think she cares?"

"She cares more than you do." Michael said.

"I took care of you after you killed our parents." Derek said. "I made sure no one knew you killed our parents and now you're going to choose some bitch that you just met, that just wants to probe you like some science rat. She's a scientist and you're choosing her over your own brother."

"Don't listen to him." I whispered to Michael from behind him. "I never lied to you. I can help you and not once have a used you as a science rat. I haven't asked you to use your power once."

"You need me Michael, not her." Derek said.

"He's wrong. You don't need him. All you need is to believe in yourself and you'll be just fine." I said.

"Whatever she is saying, she is wrong." Derek said.

"NO! YOU'RE THE ONE THAT IS WRONG!" Michael shouted. "YOU'RE THE ONE LYING!"

"Come on Mikey Mike, would I lie to you?" Derek tried to act innocent. I snorted and rolled my eyes. Hopefully Michael isn't buying any of this.

"We need to go." I said.

"Let's go back inside and we can forget this even happened." Derek said. "I'll order a pizza and we'll forget this all happened. I promise."

"Don't do it." I said. "He's lying. He will never forget it."

"Come on Michael." Derek said.

"NO!" Michael shouted. Next thing I knew Derek and most of his goons were thrown back a few feet. Without another word Michael picked up his bags and started walking the way we were heading. We walked through the small forest, going around all the trees. No one said a word. Soon we were walking into a clearing where a white van was waiting. Tony and Josh were leaning against the van with Jerry in the front seat.

"Well, good to see you two finally made it." Tony said as we approached. He took Michael's bags from him and set them into the van.

I unloaded the car before I abandoned it." Jerry said. I nodded and sat down on the floor of the van. "We thought something happened to you two. We were waiting a little bit longer before we went to look for you."

"Something did happen." I said.

"What?" Josh asked, looking at us. "What happened?"

"His brother showed up." I said. "He tried to persuade Michael into going with him."

"How?" Jerry asked.

"Well, he told Michael I am a scientist and that I just wanted Michael to be my science rat which isn't true with any of you." I said. "I have my reason to do this and I will tell you when the time is right and when I am ready." I looked at Michael as I said that.

"What did Michael do?" Josh asked.

"I flew him and his pack of jerks back a few feet before leaving with her." Michael said. Josh and Tony cheered I scolded them before turning to everyone.

"So… who's up for a road trip?"

CHAPTER 4

Mimi- What?

"THIS CANNOT BE happening." Tony said as the van made a strange noise. I pulled over to the side as the van slowly came to a stop. I opened the door and got out. I went to the front of the van and opened the hood, coughing as the smoke poured out of the car coming at me.

"Now what?" Jerry asked. "It's been hours since we saw someone, and it looks like we'll need new parts to get the van fixed."

"We walk," I said.

"What?" Josh asked. "Are you crazy?"

"Do you have a better idea?" I asked. "As Jerry pointed out we haven't seen anyone in hours. There was a sign that said there is a town in a few miles. It will be a long walk, but we can do it. It's better than just sitting here."

"You guys go right ahead. I'm staying here." Josh said, sitting on the side of the van with his arms crossed.

"Suit yourself, but you'll be all alone and just because we haven't seen a human doesn't mean other things aren't out here." I said, smirking.

Everyone but Josh got stuff together. We grabbed all our belongings that we could carry and some extra water bottles for the walk and we started to walk. After a few feet, everyone heard a howl from somewhere around us and then a van door shut, and footsteps hurried towards us. I smirked at Josh as he reached us. He rolled his eyes and we walked on.

We walked for two and a half hours before people needed a break. We found some giant rocks on the side of the road and sat down. I pulled some snacks out of my bag and passed them around as everyone pulled out water and drank. No one said anything, but the silence wasn't uncomfortable. We could hear sounds of the night. It made things calm. The sun was starting to set making everything peaceful. I watched the sky turn from blue to orange from behind the mountains. I smiled and contently got up. Peaceful break over. Everyone groaned and followed me. The walk to town started again. The boys started to get into a heated argument about who is better superhero. Josh and Michael asking questions about a lot of them. I laughed at them and walked side by side with Jerry.

A few hours after we returned to walking, we came across the outskirts of a town. A broken-down gas station was the first thing we saw. It looked like it hasn't been working in years. The pavement looked cracked and broken. The windows were broken and trash was everywhere. Everyone was looking around. Tony was kicking thing, it looked like something was wrong, but it was probably just exhaustion. I motioned to keep walking. It's late and a hotel with a bed was needed.

"Can't we just explore first?" Michael asked as we walked more into the town and more buildings could be seen.

"We just walked for hours, don't you think we should sleep and shower before exploring a random place?" Josh asked.

"When you put it that way…" Michael said.

"What other way is there? We're all dirty and tired." Tony said, laughing. I could tell he forced that laugh.

"I think we should sleep and then explore. We'd have more to explore when we are fully rested and don't smell like we haven't showered in a week." I said. "Plus, it's completely dark outside and we can't see anything."

Soon we walked into the middle of town and stood outside a bed and breakfast. It wasn't anything big or fancy, but I didn't want to walk anymore and I'm pretty sure the others don't want to keep walking either. Everyone slowly walked in. Jerry instantly walked up to the front desk where an old woman was sitting reading a book. Looking at her reminded me of the woman from the first hotel Michael and I stayed at after leaving Jamestown the first time. Everyone hung around the front door while Jerry talked to the woman. A few minutes later Jerry came over with three keys. He handed me one to me, one to the boys, and kept one for himself. Michael, Tony, and Josh must be sharing a room while Jerry and I had our own rooms. I walked up to my room, noticing the boys had a room between Jerry and me. I set my bags on my bed. I sighed greatly collapsing completely on my bed and letting exhaustion take over.

The sun hit my face, instantly waking me up. I groaned and pulled the covers over my face, hoping to get some more sleep. I shot up in the bed remembering that there are two teens and two adults waiting for me to do some exploring in this random town. I looked at the clock setting on the night stand. It read that it was almost noon. Quickly I got out of bed and into the personal bathroom connected to my bedroom. I stepped into the shower wondering if anyone else was awake or were they waiting for me.

Half an hour later I was leaving my room when I bumped into someone. I looked to see that I bumped into Michael. Next to Michael was Tony and Josh. They were all just smiling at me and not in a nice way. It was rather creepy. I started to back away, but with every step I took they took a step forward. I backed up until I hit the stairs. I would have fallen then if Michael didn't catch me.

"Are you three insane?" I asked.

"You're the one that bumped into me." Michael said, laughing as he helped me stand straight.

"I didn't know you were right outside my door." I said, walking down the steps. I could smell something good once I hit the bottom of the steps.

"We wanted to make sure you weren't going to sleep the day away." Tony said.

"We didn't want to explore without you." Josh said. I walked into the kitchen to see Jerry putting food on plates. He smiled at me as I sat down in front of a plate.

"Exploring the city since you wouldn't let us do that when we got here." Michael said. "You didn't forget, did you? We have been waiting all morning. I wanted to go wake you up, but everyone said it was rude and that I should let you sleep."

Full stomachs and backpacks full of drinks and Jerry's filled with picnic food. We were ready to go, Michael more than the rest of us. We started walking around, looking at all the buildings. They looked recently built or rebuilt. We went through every store we could find, some were vintage stores that held things built or made before anyone's time. Some were store's we knew from the places we lived before all this started. It had been a few hours now and we were starting to crave the delicious food Jerry had placed in his backpack before we left so I thought it would be time we went to the park and looked for a place to eat. As we walked the boys were all chatting away at the places we've seen and the things we looked at, all expect Tony. He was looking kind of pale and I could tell something was defiantly off and I knew it couldn't be exhaustion. Once we found a good place to sit and eat I pulled Tony aside while Josh and Michael helped Jerry set up the picnic.

"What's going on with you?" I asked once we were far enough away from everyone.

"Huh?" Tony asked, getting out of the daze he was in.

"Something is bothering you and I want to know what it is." I said. "Something has been wrong since we got here."

"I'm just tired that's all. We've been walking all day." Tony said. I was not buying it.

"Don't play games with me. I know something is wrong. You can tell me anything," I said.

"Well, you know how I can sense someone with powers right?" Tony asked.

"Yeah, I know. What does that have to do with anything?" I asked.

"I can sense someone." Tony whispered.

"Tony, that person you're sensing is Michael." I said, rolling my eyes.

"No, it's different Nicole. I am use to the feeling of his power. Everyone is different, and their feeling of their power is different, and this feeling is different." Tony said.

"What do you mean it's different?" I asked, feeling curious.

"The power I'm sensing, the feeling I'm getting... it's different then what I feel when Mikey's around which means the power is different and unless his power has changed in the last twenty-four hours someone in this town has a power and the power is strong." Tony said. He walked away without another word to join the other guys who were already munching on the food. I was no longer able to eat. My mind was focused on the strong power Tony is sensing.

The next morning, I woke up with Tony's words still on my mind. I looked at the clock next to me with it reading it was just past nine in the morning. I was tossing and turning until at least three in the morning. Could there really be powers here? Yesterday while they were eating at the park, Tony's moods were going up and down. He was fine and happy until he sensed the new power and then his mood would go way down. I got up, got dressed, and went downstairs to find only Jerry awake.

"Good, you're awake." I said, grabbing an apple from the basket in the middle of the table.

"Good morning to you too." Jerry said.

"Can you tell the boys to stay inside today?" I asked. "I have something I need to do alone and don't need to worry they are causing trouble throughout town, so I prefer it if they stayed inside."

"Does this have anything to do with Tony's mood swings since we've arrived in town?" Jerry asked.

"It might be, but I'm not sure yet." I admitted. "I'll let you know when I get back. Wish me luck."

I left the bed and breakfast, venturing into town on my own with the intent to get to the bottom of this. Being alone without the boys making random comments was quiet and weird to be honest, but I needed time alone to think things through and see if I can find them on my own. It can't be that hard. I found Michael so maybe I can find him or her too. I wasn't paying attention to where I was going I knocked into someone, knocking everything they were holding onto the ground. I felt something wet and cold go down the front of my shirt.

"Are you serious?!" the person I knocked into said in a rude tone. I could tell by her voice she was a teenager.

"I'm really sorry. I wasn't watching where I was going." I said, picking up the bags that were on the ground. I put whatever had fallen out of the bags back into the bags.

"You better be sorry. This costs more than your life. It better not be ruined!" she snapped., snatching the bags out of my hands.

"Carmen, she said she was sorry and you weren't paying attention either." Someone said. I turned around to see the same girl in different clothes. Twins.

"I don't care Caitlyn! This cost a lot of money!" Carmen said. I rolled my eyes and walked away, leaving them alone.

I walked back to the bed and breakfast and leaned on the door, sighing loudly. That did not go as well as I hoped. I couldn't find whoever had that power. Instead I ran into a spoiled rich brat. I'm going to need Tony's help after all. I'm just glad the rich girls didn't know who I am or where I am staying at or else I'd be sued for a dented handbag. I heard laughter coming from somewhere, so I followed it. I walked out into the back patio and everyone was laughing.

"Hey," Jerry said when he noticed me. "How did it go?"

"Well, I didn't find what I was looking for." I said. "Just a spoiled rich girl."

"Hey Nikki, where did you go?" Michael asked. "Jerry said you needed some girl time."

"What does that even mean? Girl time?" Josh asked. I looked at Jerry. He just shrugged his shoulders at me.

"I didn't go alone for some girl time I went alone because Tony has been sensing a power." I said.

"Well duh, I'm here." Michael said, pointing to himself.

"No, I'm use to your power." Tony said. "The power is different and it's powerful."

"More powerful than I am?" Michael asked. Tony nodded.

"What are we going to do now?" Josh asked.

"We aren't going to do anything. I am going to go out with Nicole and find that power." Tony said. He looked at me. "Right?"

"We leave after lunch." I agreed.

After lunch Tony and I left the bed and breakfast. Tony didn't say anything. He just looked around. I didn't say anything either. I didn't want to break his concentration.

"Why am I doing this again?" Tony asked after a while.

"To find whoever has the power." I said.

"But why?" Tony asked. "I still don't see or know why you're doing all this. Isn't Michael and I enough?"

It's more than just you and Michael." I said.

"Then what is it about?" Tony asked.

"That's a story for another time." I said.

"You've said that before." Tony said. "When are you going to tell us the story?"

"When I feel you are ready to hear it." I said. Tony stopped walking suddenly and I bumped into him.

"This way." Tony said, turning to the right. I followed quickly behind him.

I watched Tony. I have no idea how his power works. I tried to look up what his power means, according to the internet sensing is the ability to sense or recognize superhuman powers. Seems simple enough but looking at him it didn't seem simple. I continued to follow Tony. He looked so focused, I was so amazed by all of it. Both Tony and Michael moved differently. Michael just has a thought about moving something and it moves. Tony can feel someone who has powers and if that power is strong enough his mood will change. Like this power, whoever has it is changing his mood dramatically whenever he senses it. That's why I am looking. I need to know what it is or how it's so strong. We came to a stop at a gate.

"We're here." Tony said. "The power is behind that gate."

"Well then let's go." I said, pushing the button for the gate to be opened.

"Can I help you?" someone said from the voice box next to the buzzer.

"Um…" I said. "I'm here to speak to whoever is in charge. I have an important message from them."

The gates opened to a driveway. I started my walk up the driveway hoping Tony followed. The walk up the driveway was long, but it gave me time to think about what I was going to say. I can't just come out and tell them I have a teenager that's not mine that sensed someone in the house has a power, can I? The driveway started to get bigger as a giant mansion came into view. So, whoever has this power is either rich or could work here. A nice house like this has got to have servants. I made my way to the front door and rang the bell. It took a few minutes for someone to open the double doors. It was a maid.

"Can I help you?" she asked. I realized it was the same voice from the voice box just moments before.

"Yes, I was the one from the front gate. I'm here to see whoever is in charge here." I said. She "stepped aside and I stepped in. I noticed Tony stepped in with me.

"Wait here," the maid said before disappearing into the house. I looked around from where I stood. I could tell the owner was very rich and that this place was not designed by a man. Maybe a professional designer designed it. They could defiantly afford it.

"Can I help you?" a man's voice got my attention. I turned around. Walking down the stairs was a man in a well-dressed suit. "My maid said you wanted to see me."

"Yes, I did. My name is Nicole." I said, introducing myself. He seemed pleased.

"Well, Nicole what can I do for you?" he asked.

"Well… uh…" I started to say.

"Charles," he said, giving me his name.

"Well, Charles, is there somewhere we can go to talk privately?" I asked, looking around at all the people working.

"Sure, let's go to my office. It's this way." He said, walking past me to the right. I followed him, looking back to make sure Tony was following as well. We walked into a room I'm assuming was the office. It looked like an office. There was a desk by the window with two chairs in front of it and a couch on the other side. There was a small table near the window that held small glass cups and bottles of drinks. Charles went to the desk and sat behind it. "What is it you need to talk about so privately?"

"I'm just going to come right out and say it." I said. "I know someone in this house has some sort of power or powers."

He froze. Charles froze. I knew I caught him off guard. Not surprised. It's not something someone says to you daily. He sat there not knowing what to say to me. He started fidgeting with the things around his desk.

"I… uh…" he coughed. "I don't know what you're talking about."

"Yes, you do." I said. "I know you do. Do you want to know how I know?"

"Let's say I believe you." Charles said. "Enlighten me, tell me how you know."

"Because…" I said, looking back at Tony who was standing awkwardly by the door. "My friend Tony here can sense powers and he sensed the power that led us to this house."

"Power?" Charles asked. I could tell he was trying to play this off. "If what you say is true and he can really sense powers, it isn't just one power he is sensing. It's two."

"Two?" I asked, surprised. I wasn't expecting this.

"My daughters. Both." Charles said. "They are twins. It started with Caitlyn when she was young, and Carmen started shortly after." =

"Can I meet them?" I asked.

"You want to meet both?" he asked, shocked by my request. He looked at me for a moment. I could see he is debating if he wanted me to meet them or not. After a few minutes, he slowly nodded his head still unsure.

He got up from the chair and walked past me and out of the room, Tony quickly moving out of the way. I followed right behind him, pulling Tony with me. We followed him through his house. We went through the kitchen where there was a lot of workers running around. I was surprised when he started addressing all of them by their name, even asked some of them personal questions. Normally people like him ignored his servants.

"Wow, you have a lot of workers." I said.

"I'm hosting a dinner party for the anniversary of my late wife's birthday tomorrow night." Charles said. "She loved dinner parties so I'm throwing one in her honor."

"You knew every worker." I pointed out. "You addressed every single one of them by name and asked personal questions and things that most people like you wouldn't be able to do."

"It's my job to know every worker that comes into my home also in my work." Charles said. We got outback where six girls were lounging around a pool. "Here we are," he said. He walked a little more then stopped. "Caitlyn, Carmen, come here please."

"Coming dad!" two of the girls shouted before they got up and came towards us.

"You have got to be kidding me." I said in a muffled voice that only Tony could hear. He gave me a weird look, but I just shook my head. He did not need to know about this morning.

"Yes dad?" one of them said as they approached us.

"Someone is here to talk to you." Charles said, gesturing to me. They both looked behind Charles at me. One of the girls had a look of hatred on their face.

"What is she doing here?" she asked.

"Carmen don't be rude." Charles said. "She's here to talk to you both about your… um…" he stopped talking and looked around.

"Powers." I finished. I looked back at the other girls watching is as they waited for their friends to return. "Let's talk inside."

"Why?" Carmen asked. "Because she said so? She's the woman that ruined mu three-hundred-dollar handbag."

"It was an acc- you spent three hundred dollars on just one handbag?" I asked. "I can help. I just have some questions." I said. "I prefer to talk more privately if you don't mind."

"Let's go to my room." Caitlyn said. "No one is allowed in there without permission, so we'd be safe to talk in there."

"Lead the way." I said. She nodded her head and walked past us, leading us back into the house.

We followed Caitlyn back into the house. The kitchen got crazier. All the workers were going faster. It even looked like there were more of them. Neither of the girls said a word. Caitlyn was just walking, smiling at the workers that went by. Carmen kept her nose in the air. We walked up a marvel staircase. Everything looked like it belongs in a museum, maybe they all did. We walked down the hall until we got to a door at the end of the hall. Caitlyn opened the door and walked in. Charles and Carmen hesitated at the door. It was like they were nervous or afraid to go in. Caitlyn rolled her eyes and pulled Carmen into the room. Charles followed them in and I pulled Tony in as I walked in before closing the door.

"First things first," I said. "Introductions."

"Well, my name is Caitlyn." Caitlyn said. "Caitlyn Jackson."

"I'm Carmen." Carmen said. She doesn't seem to be warming up to me at all.

"I'm Nicole Sullivan. Dr. Nicole Sullivan." I said.

"Doctor?" Carmen scoffed. "I doubt you're a real doctor."

"What are your powers?" I asked, ignoring her. Carmen sighed and answered first.

"Well, I can negate powers." Carmen said. "Take them away."

"Is there a story behind it?" Tony asked, speaking for the first time. "Everyone has a story behind how they used theirs for the first time. I will tell you two mines sometime. I don't even think I told Nikki yet, but what are your story about how you first used your powers?"

"The only thing I remember was when I was six there was a kid named David. He was fast. It was like a blur went by when he ran. I just started thinking about how he shouldn't be able to do that and then suddenly he couldn't do it anymore. He was running like a normal person and let me tell you he runs slow when he runs like that. A few weeks went by and he was still running like a slow normal person. He was so miserable, and I felt so bad. I wanted him to have his speed back and when I did he got his speed back. So, I realized that I can take powers away, but also put them back."

"What about you?" I asked, looking at Caitlyn.

"I can mimicry. I can take in someone's power and do the same as them. I discovered mine with the same person, David." Caitlyn said.

"Where is this David?" Tony asked. He was probably thinking the same I was, he could be sensing a third power and we'd have to go looking for him.

"He passed away three years ago." Charles said. "He was hit by a drunk driver that was just here visiting while he was walking down the street."

"Oh, I'm sorry." I said.

No one said anything. For a few minutes, it was nothing but uncomfortable silence. I was looking between the two girls and thinking about how I could explain to their dad about wanting them to come with me. I might have to tell them my story, the one I have been trying to avoid. Everyone jumped when my phone went off. I pulled it out of my pocket to see an unknown number.

"Hello?" I answered. For a moment, I thought it was Michael's brother for a moment until Jerry spoke.

"Nicole, come quick. It's Michael."

CHAPTER 5

Taken by Goons

"I'M SORRY, BUT we need to go right now." I said after Jerry hung up the phone. So many thoughts were running through my head with the little information I got.

"Now? You can't leave now. We haven't finished talking. There is so much to discuss." Charles said. "Are you sure you have to leave?"

"Yes, unfortunately." I said. "There is a complication at the bed and breakfast we are staying at that I need to take care of immediately. Let's meet up for lunch or dinner before we all leave."

"Whenever that is," Tony commented. I glared at him. He backed away, almost to the door.

"Why don't you all come to the dinner party tomorrow night? I'm sure we can move something around, so you and all your friends can come. How many are with you?" Charles asked.

"There are five all together." I said. "There is another besides Tony that I would like your daughters to meet, but he doesn't have the same power. His is something different."

"Five is fine. We can defiantly make the room." Charles said. "The party is tomorrow at seven. I hope that is alright."

"Seven is fine." I said. "See you there." I walked away, dragging Tony with me.

"What's going on?" Tony asked when we got outside and down the driveway, walking away from the house.

"Something is wrong with Michael." I said, focusing on getting back to the bed and breakfast.

"What do you mean something is wrong with Michael?" Tony asked.

"I don't know. Jerry said come quick it's Michael and then hung up before I could get a word out." I said. "Did you feel something change?" I asked. Tony shook his head.

"What do you think is wrong?" Tony asked as the bed and breakfast started to come into view.

"I don't know. Whatever it is I'm hoping his brother isn't involved." I said as we got closer to the bed and breakfast.

We got to the bed and breakfast and I hurried up the stairs thinking they'd be in one of the rooms, but no one was in any of the rooms we booked. I went back downstairs looking everywhere to find everyone in the dining room waiting for me. Tony had joined them. His face wasn't puzzled. He looked more like he was amused. I immediately went to Michael and looked him over.

"*I'm fine.*" I heard Michael say, but I was staring at his face at the time. I didn't see his lips move.

"What did you just say?" I asked, thinking that maybe I blinked and just didn't see his lips move when he talked.

"*I said I'm fine.*" I heard Michael say. I was staring at his lips the whole time without blinking. His lips did not move.

"It's finally happening. I'm going insane." I said. "I am going freaking insane. This cannot be happening right now."

"*No, you're not. Chill out.*" I heard Michael say.

"Stop that! Right now!" I snapped. Michael chuckled and put his hands up in defense. I turned to everyone else.

"Tony and I found the people behind the sensing and Tony's mood swings. It was twins which explains why it was so strong." I said, trying to change the subject.

"Twins?" Jerry asked, surprised. "Are you sure?"

"Yes twins." I confirmed. "Tomorrow you will all meet them at a dinner party hosted by their father, so I want you all to wear your best clothes."

"What if we don't have any best clothes? What if what we are wearing is our best clothes?" Tony asked with Josh nodding along with him.

"I can help with that. I've got plenty of money that just sits there so I can help." Jerry said. I looked at him. He smiled at me in reassurance.

"Why don't we all go shopping and get something to wear?" I suggested. Everyone cheered. "Everyone like the plan then?" I laughed. "Let's get ready to go then." Everyone got up, including Michael. I stopped him. "Everyone except you. Sit back down. We need to talk."

Michael sat back down. "Alright, let's talk."

"What happened?" I asked.

"It was nothing really." Michael said. "We were all sitting here waiting for you and Tony to get back when I got hungry, so I had some fries made. As I was eating them I thought about how they could use some salt."

"Where is this going?" I asked.

"Without a word Jerry handed me the salt." Michael said.

"What does salt have to do with anything? He could have just thought you needed salt for the fries." I said.

"That's what I thought then Josh asked him why he handed me the salt." Michael said. "Jerry said I told him I needed the salt, but Josh said he didn't hear me say anything, so I tested something out by thinking something else. I thought about how Josh's feet smell. He said out loud that they do not. Jerry looked confused by his outburst. I asked Jerry if he knew what I said, and he said he didn't."

"So, not only are you telepathic, but you can tell people things with your mind. That's just wonderful." I said sarcastically.

"That's not all I can do." Michael said cheerfully.

"What?" I asked in confusion. Michael got excited and jumped out of his chair.

"Here, come on, sit down." Michael said. I did what he said and sat down in the chair. Michael sat down in front of me. Michael looked at me and not in the admiration kind of way, but in the kind of way that creeps me out. I was about to say something to Michael when something made my eyes go blind that I couldn't see anything.

"Michael?! Where are you?!" I saw what looks like a young Derek say. He was looking for someone. "Michael!" he shouted as he ran up to a little boy. "There you are! I've been looking everywhere for you! Why did you run off like that?"

"Uncle Jack hates me." Little Michael said. "Our whole family hates me."

"Why do you think that?" the young Derek asked. "There has to be a reason you think that. You were fine this morning before the funeral when we were alone in the house. What happened?"

"I heard Uncle Jack. He said I am the reason that mommy and daddy aren't here anymore." Little Michael said. You could see the tears going down his face.

"Don't listen to him Mikey." Derek said. "He's wrong. It wasn't your fault. It wasn't anyone's fault."

"He told Aunt Sue that if it wasn't for me they wouldn't be a funeral and they'd still be with us." Michael said. Derek pulled Michael onto his lap and held him.

"Michael listen to me," Derek said, grabbing Michael by his shoulders and made him look at him. "You are not the cause of our parents dying. It was an accident. Mom and dad wouldn't want you to blame yourself no matter what anyone says."

"I miss them." Michael said. "Do you think they are happy where they are? Are they together?" Michael asked.

"Yes, they are together. I think they are happy watching down on us." Derek said. "Now come on let's leave everyone and go to the movies."

"What in the world was that?" I asked when my sight came back, and I could see again. I looked at Michael to see him smiling. "What the hell did you do to me?"

"I just showed you one of my memories." Michael said. He looked as though he felt accomplished for something.

"That was a memory?" I asked, shocked by what I saw.

"It was the day we buried our parents and the last time I saw anyone from my family. Anyone besides Derek. No one wanted to see me again. Derek might have told the police a lie about my parent's death, but my family knew I did it and wanted nothing to do with me." We were interrupted by Tony coming back into the room.

"Are we going shopping or what?" Tony asked. I laughed and looked at Michael.

"Yes. I think shopping is what we all need." I said, getting up and walking out of the room.

We all left the bed and breakfast, using a taxi this time so Jerry wasn't walking all the way to the mall. The taxi ride only took ten minutes. We got out, I paid the driver, and we entered the mall. The mall wasn't that big. It had a couple major stores with a few small ones and a small food court mainly sold pizza in varied sizes. I watched as Tony, Josh, and Michael walk off together laughing and talking, leaving Jerry and I alone. We started walking our own way to a store.

"Did you see the twins use their power?" Jerry asked, looking at me. "Was it as amazing as the boys using theirs?"

"I haven't seen it yet. We were just talking when you called." I said. "I am hoping we can see something at the dinner party tomorrow night."

"What is this dinner party for?" Jerry asked.

"According to him it is for the anniversary of his late wife's birthday." I said.

We walked into the only dress store I saw. There was rows and rows of dresses on one side and rows and rows of suits on the other. Jerry went to the side with the suits. I started browsing through the dresses. They were beautiful, but too elegant for a dinner party and they were a lot pricier. Maybe something elegant would be nice after everything that has happened or will happen since I doubt Derek is done until he gets Michael back under his control. I continued to look, not really liking anything until I came across a blue dress, it was a light blue dress. It was short, just a little above the knee with most of the back showing. It was gorgeous and in my budget.

"You should get it," two voices said in unison from behind me. I turned to see Michael and Josh standing behind me with bags in their hands. Tony wasn't with them. They came over to stand next to me, both looking at the dress.

"I think I will." I said, smiling. I walked up to the register to pay for the dress. Jerry was already there paying for his suit. I did the mistake of looking through the glass windows that can show who is in the hallway near the store. "Michael," I said in a stern voice. He came over to me with Josh right behind him.

"What is it?" Michael asked. I pointed to the man standing on the other side of the glass, staring at us with a smirk on his face. He had to be one of Derek's goons. I looked around to see four more walking around the area but looking this way with the same smirk on their faces.

"Well, it could be your brother's goons hanging outside waiting for us to leave." I said. "Where is Tony?" I asked.

"We left him in the store. He was trying on clothes muttering something about impressing someone named Carmen." Michael said. "He said he shouldn't be much longer. He's probably done by now."

"Where is the store?" I asked.

"About four stores down, just past the food court." Josh said. I looked from the goon to the woman who was ringing up the dress. I could tell she was trying not to pay attention to our conversation.

"Excuse me ma'am." I said to the woman. She looked at me. "Is there a back door we can go out? That man looking in, he is my ex-husband and I just really want to avoid running into him. He was not a good man." She looked back at the goon and turned back to me.

"I see what you mean. He doesn't look nice." She said. "I can get in trouble for this. Past the changing rooms. Third door on the right. They are double doors with the emergency exit sign in red on top."

"Thank you." I said. I looked at Michael and Josh. "We need to get Tony." I paid for the dress and we backed up a few steps. The goon that was looking into the store through the glass came in.

"Hello Michael," the goon said. Michael sighed. "Care to introduce us?"

"Everyone, this is Nathan. My brother's main idiot." Michael said. "How did you find me?"

"Last time we got you back your brother and I knew that the little missy here wouldn't stay away. We knew she'd come back for you like the stupid woman she is. So, we put a tracker on you so that he'd know where she takes you and we can bring you back." Nathan said.

"YOU PUT A TRACKER ON ME?!" Michael shouted. Nathan smirked. "I know you didn't implant it. My brother isn't smart enough to have that done by anyone and I know it's not in my clothes." Nathan chuckled.

"You are wearing the new shoes he got you, aren't you?" Nathan asked. Michael looked down at his feet and with a quick motion, he took off his shoes. Michael looked at me, then to Josh, and then back to Nathan.

"On the count of three, I want you all to run." Michael said.

"But Michael-" I started to say.

"One..." Michael said.

"Nicole, does he really expect us all to run?" Jerry asked.

"Two..." Michael said. I could see he was set on something. Whatever it was, it can't be good.

"No Jerry, just stay here." I said. The woman who rang up my dress pulled Jerry aside and made him sit in a chair behind her. I gave Jerry the dress for safe keeping.

"THREE!" Michael shouted, throwing the shoes one by one at Nathan as hard as he could. One hit him in the face and the other hit him in the gut, making him bend over. I took the opportunity the run around Nathan and into the hallway. "NICOLE DON'T!" I heard Michael shout as he came after me, but it was too late.

They already saw me.

"Well... well... well..." one of the goons in the hallway said. "Nicole isn't it?"

"Back off Mack." I heard Michael say from behind me.

"No one is talking to you Mikey." The goon Michael called Mack said. He turned back to me. "Now, where were we? Oh yeah, Nicole, right?"

"Uh, no?" I tried to say, but it came out more like a question.

"Oh, I think you are." He said. "You just ran out of there."

"How do you know I wasn't just shopping and the big guy just scared me and that's why I ran out of there?" I asked. I watched Josh and Jerry walk around everyone and walk towards a shocked Tony standing a few feet away. I watched as they pulled him away. Where is Michael?

"Didn't Mikey just call you by your name?" he asked. "And tell me to back off."

"No?" I said, but once again it was more like a question.

"Let's pretend I believe you." He said. He came towards me along with the other around. Mack smirked, and I was hit hard.

Everything went dark.

I woke up with my head pounding. I couldn't see anything. Something was on my head and by the smell of it, it was a potato sack. My hands were also tied behind my back. There was some noise around me. At least I know I'm not alone, wherever I am. From the sound of it someone was watching television and people were playing cards. The only thought I currently have is if the others were safe, but also how many goons were in the room with me. I need to get free and get to the others.

"Do you think she's awake yet?" someone asked.

"No idea. Mack hit her pretty hard," someone answered.

"She was smart mouthing me," someone said. I remember that voice, it was Mack talking.

"She wasn't smart mouthing you. She just lied to you." Someone else answered. So far, I can tell there are at least four people in the room with me.

"Quiet!" someone snapped. It sounded like the first guy that talked. "She could be awake and listening."

"One way to find out." I heard Mack say. I heard a chair scrape across the floor and footsteps came towards me.

The potato sack was yanked off my head. I looked up to see Mack standing there with the sack in his hand. He had a smirk on his face that I didn't like.

"Well, hello there." Mack said in a very creepy voice. "You're finally awake. We've been waiting for you."

"Can I help you?" I asked sarcastically.

"Your sarcasm is noted," someone said. It was coming from the one still at the table in the room. It was the first time he spoke.

"Oh, it's there." I said, rolling my eyes.

"Listen here princess," he said, getting up and coming over to me.

"Do I look like a princess to you?" I asked, annoyed. He didn't answer me. I felt his hand hit the right side of my face. The sting on my face made me whimper. My hands were tied behind my back, but I still had the urge to touch the part of my face that he hit.

"Hey!" Mack said to the hitter. "D doesn't want her injured. He said to leave the bitch alone until he comes back with Mikey." I hope they didn't find him.

"Well, he's not here so I say we have a little fun with the bitch that has caused all of us problems for weeks and why D has been in a shitty mood for weeks." He said. Everyone cheered. "If anyone has a problem with it, they can join her." He looked at Mack who gulped and backed away.

No one said anything. No one helped me.

It felt like it was forever until they were done with me. Punching, hitting, kicking wherever their hands or feet landed. By the time they were done, my eyes were swollen that I couldn't see anything. I have no idea how bad my body looked.

"WHAT DID I SAY ABOUT NOT TOUCHING HER!" I heard Derek shout when he came in. I couldn't see him, but I could defiantly hear his voice.

"She… um… mouthed off so we gave her a lesson," someone said.

"I TOLD YOU ALL TO CAPTURE HER AND HOLD HER NOT TO TORTURE HER!" Derek shouted. "THIS ISN'T GOING TO GET ME CLOSE TO MICHAEL!"

"We didn't do anything that bad," he said.

"THAT BAD?! SHE LOOKS LIKE SHE WAS DRAGGED ACROSS THE PAVEMENT A FEW TIMES!" Derek shouted at them. I couldn't tell where anyone was, but it sounded like Derek was close to me.

"And here I thought I was looking pretty being tired up and beaten." I said. "I bet I'm still better looking than you."

"Everyone out!" Derek snapped. "Go help the others find Mikey." I heard footsteps as everyone left.

"So, you haven't found him?" I asked, relieved. I felt something wet and warm touch my face.

"Where is he?" Derek asked.

"How am I supposed to know?" I asked. "Besides if you've had the tracker on him the whole time then you should have known this entire time where we are and where we've been staying."

Derek didn't respond.

After a while of warm dabs on my face and I could finally start to see. I was right. Derek was sitting right in front of me. He continued to dab my face with the warm cloth, cleaning the cloth in a small bucket a few times. We sat in the quiet for a while as he continued to clean up what his goons did to me. Soon the pain sustained, and I could start blinking again. When I started blinking again Derek stopped with the cloth.

"I will find him." Derek said. He untied me and got up, leaving the front door wide open as he left. I looked myself over. There were bruises all over my arms and legs. I looked out the open door. I didn't know if anyone is coming back, but I took this chance and slowly got up. I was sore in a lot of places, but I could not let it hold me back. I need to get back to the bed and breakfast. I know that they couldn't find Michael, but what about the others? Are they safe?

The walk back to the bed and breakfast took me most of the night. I started walking at maybe one or two in the morning and the sun was starting to ride in the distance when the bed and breakfast came into view. I slowly walked up to the bed and breakfast and walked inside. I looked around as I closed the front door. Jerry was asleep on the couch in the living room. I walked over and shook him away. He blinked a few times before looking at me.

"Nicole?" Jerry asked, surprised to see me. I nodded my head. "Thank goodness you're alright." He quickly got up.

"Where are the boys? Are they alright?" I asked. "Where's Michael? Did they get him?" Jerry put his hand up to stop me.

"Everyone is fine." Jerry said. He walked to the bottom of the stairs. "BOYS! COME DOWN! SHE'S BACK!"

I heard footsteps bouncing down the stairs like a herd of stampedes as they hurried down.

"NICOLE!" Josh and Tony shouted in unison. I smiled at them. I looked up at Michael who was standing in the back, a few steps above the boys. He eyed me up and down as he gulped.

"I'm fine." I said to Michael. He smiled at me, but I knew it was fake. It didn't reach his eyes.

"What happened?" Tony asked.

"We watched them knock you unconscious and take you." Josh said. "We tried to follow, but we lost them. We looked for you until Jerry wouldn't let us anymore."

"Well, I woke up with a sack on my head and my hands tied behind my back." I said. "They beat me until Derek showed up." I looked up at Michael. "He was the one that let me go."

"What?" Michael looked shocked. "Are we talking about the same Derek?"

"Yes." I said. Michael shook his head and walked down the steps until he was right in front of me.

"That doesn't sound like my brother." Michael said.

"I know, but it's the truth." I said. I walked over to the couch and sat down for the first time since I left the place I was being held at. Jerry came over with a first aid kit and started attending to my wounds. Watching him made me miss Arthur.

"Well, we're packed and ready to hit the road." Tony said. "We even packed your stuff."

"What are you talking about?" I asked as I looked up at him.

"They had a tracker on him." Jerry said, gesturing to Michael with his head as his hands were full. "They know where we are so we're leaving aren't we?"

"We can't go." I said. They all looked at me like I was going crazy.

"Why not?" Jerry asked.

"We still have a dinner party to go to if they really knew where we were they would have taken him by now." I said. They all looked at each other. "What?"

"You look like… well… roadkill." Michael said.

"Your brother called it being dragged down the pavement a few times." I said. "Anyway, we are still going. End of discussion."

It was almost six. Charles is expecting us at seven. I was sitting on the bed. With everything that has happened, I don't have the dress I paid for. I sighed I was about to go through my bag to see if I had anything that would be good for a dinner party when a knock was at the door. Before I could say anything or answer the door, the door opened, and Michael came in. He came in with a bag in his arms. It was the dress. Michael put it on the bed and left the room without another word. I walked over and took the dress out of the bag before going to the bathroom to get ready. I hope everyone else is getting ready.

We walked up the driveway, all the trees were decorated with lights leading up to the house. The house looked more amazing then when I was last here. Walking up to the door, I could hear people inside talking. I started to get nervous as I pushed the doorbell. How am I going to explain how I look to all these people I don't even know? The doors opened, and Charles stood in the doorway.

"Nicole? Something… what…" Charles said, lost for words as he looked at me up and down just like Michael did when he first saw me. He shook his head and recomposed himself. "Nicole! Good to see you again!"

"Hello Charles," I said, relieved he didn't question anything.

"The girls will be happy to know you made it." Charles said. "They were worried we scared you away."

"I don't scare that easily." I said. I pointed to Tony. "You remember Tony don't you Charles?"

"Yes, I do." Charles said. He took out his hand for Tony to shake it. "How are you son?"

"I'm good sir." Tony said, shaking Charles' hand.

"These are the others that are with me." I said.

"Do they... are they all like my daughters?" Charles asked. "You know... powers?" Charles whispered. I laughed.

"No. Besides Tony just Michael does." I said, pointing to Michael.

"So, what do they do?" Charles asked, pointing at Josh and Jerry.

"They are more like my helpers." I said. "This is Josh and Jerry." I pointed to each as I introduced them.

"Well, come in. All of you." Charles moved aside so we can all come in. "The girls are out by the pool. I've got to go find someone. I'll be there in a moment." Charles pointed in the direction to go and walked away from us, more into the house. I went the way he pointed.

"Hey girls!" I called when I saw them. They were both in pretty dresses, talking to each other.

"NICOLE!" they screamed in unison. "YOU CAME BACK!"

"Yes, I did." I laughed at their excitement as they came running up to me. "And I brought the rest of my friends with me. Girls, this is Michael, Josh, and Jerry," I said, pointing to each one as I introduced them to the girls. "You remember Tony don't you girls?"

"Yes, we do." Carmen said. "Hey Tony."

"Hi," Tony said quietly. Tony blushed and hid behind Michael. I laughed out loud.

"Guys, this is Caitlyn and Carmen. The twins I was telling you about." I said, making sure I knew to point out who is who so no one got confused. "We have a conversation to finish."

CHAPTER 6

The Past Can Always Come Back

O N THE POOL deck in the corner sat a fire pit that took advantage of. Caitlyn got one of the maids to go out and bring us chocolate, graham crackers, and giant marshmallows. Caitlyn was staring at Michael. Not in the adoration kind of way, but in the kind of way like she was studying him. Michael kept making smores, not having any notice to Caitlyn's stares. A moment later I watched as a piece of wood came up in the air and landed on the dying fire, making the fire come to life without anyone touching it. I looked around to see everyone staring from the fire to Michael.

"Michael," I said in a warning tone. He wasn't supposed to do that.

"It wasn't me," he said, putting his chocolate covered hands in the air.

"It was me." Caitlyn said. "I haven't done that in a while."

"Not since David." Carmen commented. I looked between the twins.

"Can one of you explain this to me?" I asked. Carmen and Caitlyn raised her hand.

"I started it." Carmen said. "Ever since you told us what Tony can do, I wanted to try my power out. While you guys were here yesterday I tested it out on Tony." Carmen eyed Tony.

"What do you mean you tested your power out on me?" Tony asked, surprised.

"I kind of took your power away to test if I could still do it." Carmen said. "I can't use the power. I can only take it away."

I looked at Tony. "Did you feel different at any time while we were with them?" I asked.

"Now that I think about it while we were in the bedroom and the girls were explaining their powers to you, I lost my sensing for their powers and Michael's, but then it came back so I let it go. I didn't think anything of it." Tony said.

"That was me." Carmen said.

"Continue." I said. I looked at Carmen expecting her to answer, but Caitlyn answered.

"When you guys arrived tonight, I wanted to test mine out, so I did what Carmen did and tested it out on Tony." Caitlyn said.

"HEY!" shouted Tony.

"After I got Tony's power I felt it," Caitlyn said. "I felt Michael's power through Tony's. I felt how strong it is, how powerful. Is it always like that?"

"Pretty much," Tony said. "The only time I've ever felt it weakened was when he's been injured."

"After I felt Michael's power I wanted to try it out." Caitlyn said. "Not as a power-crazy kind of way, but more out of curiosity."

"That's why you were staring at him so hard. You were taking his power." I said.

"My question is, how did you know what to do?" Michael said.

"Michael has a point. We haven't talked about his power." I said. Caitlyn looked at Michael.

"You are telepathic." Caitlyn said.

"What does that mean?" Carmen asked.

"He moves things with his mind." Caitlyn said. "There's something else like another power, but I can't figure it out."

"I can put things into people's minds." Michael said. "Can I have my power back now?"

"You had your power the whole time I just copied it." Caitlyn said. Michael lifted a piece of wood and placed it in the fire pit, making it come to life again. "I can just make it, so I don't have the power anymore."

"CARMEN!" I heard Tony shout. I looked to see Carmen looking away. "Give me my power back."

"Carmen, give the boy his power back." Charles said as he approached.

"Fine." Carmen said, crossing her arms.

"Charles, I didn't hear you coming." I said.

"I could tell." Charles said. I noticed someone was standing slightly behind Charles. He wasn't wearing a suit which pretty much all the men at the dinner party were wearing so he must not have been there, but he was still kind of dressy.

"I'm Thomas, but I prefer to be called Tommy," he introduced himself. "It's what our mom loved to call me."

"TOMMY!" the girls shouted in unison. They got up and ran to him.

"Hey girls," Tommy said. "How were your midterms?"

"Aced!" They said together. Tommy laughed.

"I thought so." Tommy said.

"Nicole, I was hoping we could finish talking." Charles said.

"Sure." I said. Charles and Tommy made themselves comfortable around the fire pit. Tommy picked up at fire poker and began making smores. "What do you want to talk about?"

"Well, as you should be aware. I had you looked into just like I do with everyone that comes into my family's life." Charles said. I looked at him.

"You… uh… you what?" I asked.

"You should have known with a man like myself that I would have you and your entire family looked into." Charles said.

"Did you find something worth talking about?" I asked.

"Ethan Jacob Sullivan." Charles said.

I gulped.

He said the one name I hoped he didn't find. My little brother.

"Nicole, who is he talking about?" Jerry asked, but I couldn't answer him. I couldn't answer anyone. My throat was completely dry. It felt like it was closing in.

"Breathe," someone said. I looked to see Tommy now sitting beside me. "Breathe," he said again. I took some deep breaths as Tommy rubbed my back.

"What's going on with her?" I heard Carmen ask, but I didn't look at her. I closed my eyes and tried to focus on breathing.

"She's having a panic attack." Tommy said. "She'll be fine once she calms down."

I kept my eyes closed. It felt like hours before I could finally breathe again, and my throat wasn't so dry. I opened my eyes to everyone staring at me with different expressions on their faces.

"I didn't mean to cause you to have a panic attack. I'm sorry." Charles said. He looked really concerned.

"I wasn't expecting you to say that name." I admitted.

"What's wrong with the name?" Tony asked.

"Nothing is wrong with the name." I said. "I picked it. It's just... a very long story."

"We have time." Michael said, putting his hand on my knee.

"I have never talked about this with anyone, so I don't think I can." I admitted.

"Cliff notes." Tommy encouraged.

"Cliff notes." I repeated Tommy, nodding to myself. I took a few breaths and closed my eyes before I started to speak. "His name is Ethan and he is my little brother."

"Little brother?" Michael asked. "You have a little brother?"

"Had." I corrected.

"What do you mean 'had'?" Charles asked. "There wasn't a death certificate. Just a birth certificate."

"You won't find one." I said. "He isn't dead."

"I'm confused." Caitlyn said. "If he isn't dead then how can you say you had a brother?"

"I haven't seen him since he was four." I said.

"Why not?" Michael asked. "Did you parents hate him or something?"

"MICHAEL!" Tommy and Charles shouted together. I ignored it.

"No, they didn't hate him." I said. "The complete opposite. They loved him."

"I'm not following you." Tony said.

"He was an empath." I said.

"A what?" Michael asked.

"What's an empath?" Caitlyn asked.

"What do they do?" Carmen asked.

"An empath is someone who can not only sense someone's emotions, but also feel it themselves." I explained. "Say you're in pain, it could be for any reason and if an empath was anywhere near you then they'd feel that exact pain you feel."

"So, if I had something as simple as a toothache they'd feel that too? Or even a headache?" Carmen asked.

"Yes," I said simply. Everyone went silent.

"What happened to him?" Caitlyn asked after a few minutes of silence.

"They gave him up to a secluded place where he could be free without having to feel anyone's pain." I said.

"Do you miss him?" Carmen asked.

"Yeah, do you miss him?" a voice said. Everyone looked around to see someone standing in the darkness.

"No. No. No. No. No." Michael said. He was shaking his head as someone came into the light for everyone to see.

Derek.

I quickly stood up and took a stance in front of Michael. Not that it did anything he's taller than me.

"Get out of here Derek. You can't have him." I said. Derek chuckled.

"You think so? I think you'll change your mind when you see what I have." Derek said. "Or rather who I have."

"What are you talking about? I would never give you your brother." I said. Tony and Tommy joined my side to protect Michael.

"Not even for your own brother?" Derek asked, smirking.

"I have no idea what you're talking about." I said, my voice cracking as I spoke.

"Don't lie. Lying is unattractive." Derek said.

"I'm not lying." I said.

"I know you are. Do you know the reason I let you go?" Derek asked.

"Because deep down you have a heart?" I guessed. Derek laughed.

"Not even close." Derek said. "Actually, I let you go because I knew you'd lead me right to my brother."

"It doesn't matter, you're still not getting him." I said. "There's nothing you can say or do to change that."

"You think so?" Derek asked. I nodded. "What if I told you the rich guy isn't the only one that can look someone up?"

"What are you talking about?" I asked.

"Like old man rivers, I know about your brother Ethan." Derek said. "But unlike him I did something about it. I found him."

"What did you do?" Michael asked.

"Oh boys," Derek said. Out of the shadows, two of his goons stepped out of the darkness, but they weren't alone. In between the two being held by the arms by them was a kid who looked to be fourteen. Derek smirked at me.

"Who's that?" Michael asked.

"You don't recognize him Nicole?" Derek asked, looking at me. "You should. He's your brother."

"What?" I asked, looking at the boy. "He's my… you…" I couldn't make words. I looked from him to Derek then back to the kid.

"Nicole, who is the kid?" Jerry asked.

"Ethan?" I asked, my eyes not moving from the kid.

"Yes? Who are you?" he asked, looking at me.

"I- um…" I started to say but stopped. I have no idea how I would explain anything. "Charles, maybe you should let your dinner guests know it's time to go."

"Maybe, you're right." Charles said. He walked around everyone and went inside. Tommy moved to stand in front of the girls.

"Why is there so much anger?" Ethan asked.

"What do you say Nicole?" Derek asked. "Your brother for my brother?"

"Never." I said.

"You would choose my brother over your own?" Derek asked.

"Brother?" Ethan asked, looking at Derek. "Who's brother?"

"That would be her." Derek said, pointing directly at me. "You are her brother."

"What are you talking about?" Ethan asked. He looked at me. "What does he mean I'm your brother?"

"Don't listen to him." I said.

"But why is he saying I'm your brother?" Ethan asked. 'And seriously what's with all the anger? I feel like my head is going to explode."

"Carmen." I said. She looked at me. "Power. Ethan. Now."

Carmen nodded at me. She looked at Ethan. I looked back at Ethan. His posture changed. It went from looking angry to looking normal. As if there was no anger at all. I sighed in relief.

"What just happened?" Derek asked, looking from Carmen to Ethan.

"You were hoping one of two things would have happened. One, I would trade Ethan for Michael or two Ethan would feel all the anger we feel for you and make everyone explode or something."

"You can't prove that." Derek said. I rolled my eyed. I know where this was just about to go. I looked at Tommy who was still just protecting the girls. I could feel Tony next to me and Michael right behind me. Jerry stood off to the side, standing alone. I looked back at Derek. He was looking at Jerry with a smirk on his face.

"Derek don't do this." Michael said, stepping around me. I tried to grab him, but Tony held me back. "You don't need to hurt anyone else."

"Don't I?" Derek asked. "Are you telling me you're going to come quietly?"

"Derek, I am not your monkey." Michael said. "You just want me for my power to make people scared of you."

"What do you think she wants from you?" Derek asked.

"She hasn't made me use my power against people once since I met her." Michael said. Derek scuffed.

"Just wait little bro, eventually everyone shows their true colors." Derek said. "It's your choice. Either you come with me or you don't, but if you choose the wrong choice there will be consequences."

Michael shook his head. "No." Everyone stood in silence, looking at Derek. He slid his hand across his mouth. You could tell he was disappointed.

"This isn't over." Derek said. "Come on boys."

Derek walked away, walking into the house. I thought for a moment that for once everything turned out in our favor, but then I remembered that nothing that has happened turned out in our favor. I was about to turn to Michael and Tony who were now standing side by side when I heard it. The sound of something being ripped and I heard a groan. I turned around to see one of the goons pulling a knife out of Jerry's abdomen. He smirked at me and walked away, taking the bloody knife with him. I stood there in shock as Jerry fell to his knees and then falling backwards onto his back. It was like he moved in slow motion, slow painful motion. Without another word I ran over to Jerry and pushed my hand onto his wound to try to stop the bleeding. He was bleeding so bad that my hands were covered with blood in a matter of seconds. They had gotten an artery. I looked around silently, hoping for someone to help me. Everyone was standing there shocked, all but Tommy. Tommy was on his phone talking to someone, having people get here to help Jerry. Michael came back to life from his shocked trance and set into gear. He took off his jacket and placed it over my hands, taking over trying to stop the bleeding. I went to the other end of Jerry where his head lay on the ground. Tears were streaming down my face, I could hardly see.

"Hold on Jerry. Help is on the way. You've just got to hold on." I said, placing his head onto my lap.

"Nicole…" Jerry started to say. I stopped him.

"Shh. Just hold on." I said.

"Nicole…" Jerry said again. I looked down at him. "I'm not going to make it."

"Don't say that." I said. "You can't say that. You're going to make. You are going to be just fine."

"No, I won't." Jerry said. "I can feel it."

"No. I don't believe it." I said. "I won't."

"Nicole, I just want you to know I enjoyed meeting you." Jerry said. I couldn't see anything anymore with all the tears streaming down my face.

"No. Don't do this. You cannot go anywhere." I said. "You can't leave me with all the boys. I won't allow it."

"Nicole…" Jerry said slowly. I waited for Jerry to say something, but he didn't. Instead, his eyes closed, and he slowly stopped breathing. Everything stopped.

CHAPTER 7

The Long Goodbye

I WATCHED AS JERRY'S blood went down the drain as I stood in the shower. I didn't move. I couldn't move. I just let the water fall down my body, taking the blood with it. It's only been a few hours since Jerry was killed. The ambulance got there a few moments too late. He died right there. He died in front of me with his head on my lap. He died because of me.

A knock of my door snapped me out of my trance. I quickly turned the water off, not caring if the blood was all off me and got out, wrapping a towel around myself before going to the door to open it.

"Hey," Josh said. I smiled slightly as I stood there, naked in nothing, but a towel.

"I was taking a shower." I said. "What do you need?"

"We thought you shouldn't be alone tonight." Josh said.

"We?" I asked, raising an eyebrow. Josh rolled his eyes and pulled someone next to him. It was Michael. "Is Tony going to appear too?"

"Maybe," Tony said, coming to the other side of Josh.

"All of you stay there. Let me get some clothes on." I said. I shut the door without letting them say anything. I quickly got dressed and let them back in. "What do you all expect to do?"

"Well," Michael said. "None of us wanted to be alone tonight and we defiantly didn't think you should be alone."

"I'm fine." I lied. "I'll be alright to be alone."

"Isn't that girl code for you are not fine?" Tony asked. "Anyway, we rented a whole bunch of movies and the twins didn't want to be alone at their house, so we invited them, and they are bringing drinks and snacks."

"And I ordered pizza. It should be here soon." Josh said.

"You guys don't really need to do this." I said. To be honest, this was probably something I needed.

"Maybe we don't, but we're doing it anyway." Michael said. There was a knock on the door. "That is either the girls or the pizza." It was both.

Half an hour later, there was pizza boxes scattered on the floor, some half eaten, some not touched. Michael had picked some horror movie, but I think he picked that for a reason or at least someone helped him pick it out. He probably didn't pick it alone. Both Michael and Tony jumped at the idea of watching a horror movie, they both even situated everything so that the twins sat between them. Everyone jumped when there was a knock on the door.

"I'll get it," I said since I wasn't really into watching the movie. I got up from the bed and answered the door. "Tommy, what are you doing here?"

"My dad said my sisters were here and asked if I would check on them." Tommy said. "Plus, I didn't think you should be alone."

"I'm not alone." I said, looking back at the boys and the twins. "Apparently no one thought I should be alone."

"They are all on the floor." Tommy pointed out, looking at them. "I'm sure you could use someone to sit with." Tommy smiled at me.

"Come on! Let him in!" Carmen shouted from her position next to Tony on the floor. I moved aside and let Tommy in. He took off the coat he was wearing and his shoes before getting onto my bed. He patted the spot next to him, the exact spot I was just lying.

"I promise I don't bite." Tommy said. "And if I do, I promise I've had all my shots." I rolled my eyes and joined him on the bed. I leaned against the bed post, keeping my distance. Well, I tried to. Tommy moved himself to be right next to me, leaning on the bed post as well. I tried to concentrate on the movie, but since I wasn't paying attention at the beginning of the movie I have no idea what is going on or who is chasing who or even why. Apparently, it's scary though since both twins are jumping into Michael and Tony's arms.

After the horror movie, the twins got to pick the next movie. They picked something they brought, a romantic comedy. All the boys groaned as the movie started, making me laugh. That's what they get for letting teenage girls pick a movie.

"I think that's enough for me." I said, getting up. I grabbed my shoes. "I'm going to take a walk. You all enjoy your movies. Clean up when you're done."

"Do you want some company?" Tommy asked, coughing a little. "You know in case his brother is still out there. Two is better than one." I thought for a moment while everyone stared.

"Yeah, sure. That would be great." I said. Tommy smiled and got up so fast that he fell over. "Josh, make sure they don't try anything." I gestured to Tony and Michael.

"You got it boss." Josh said. I grabbed a coat and left the room with Tommy.

"You don't think they are going to try anything with my sisters, do you?" Tommy asked as we left the bed and breakfast and started down the street.

"I don't think you need to worry about Michael." I said. "Tony on the other hand... I'm not sure."

"He better not try anything if he knows what is good for him." Tommy said. I laughed, and everything went silent. We walked together in silence, but it wasn't awkward. It was quite nice. "Listen," Tommy said after a while. "I'm sorry about your friend."

"Thanks." I said slowly.

"How well did you know him?" Tommy asked.

"Not that well." I said. "I met him when I was trying to help Michael get away from his brother. He helped me when I got injured."

"How did he do that?" Tommy asked.

"Uh, he brought me to a friend of his that was a retired doctor." I said. We walked until we were met with some sand. I walked until I was hitting water and sat down, setting my legs and feet into the water. Tommy followed.

"Where is his friend?" Tommy asked.

"What is this, twenty questions?" I snapped.

"I'm sorry," Tommy said, looking out. I sighed.

"No, I'm sorry." I said. "You're just asking a lot of questions."

"I didn't think you'd tell me anything if I didn't ask." Tommy admitted. He looked at me.

"You're probably right." I said.

I looked out into the water as silence took over, awkward silence. My mind was swimming with so many thoughts. How could Derek do something like this? Just kill someone in cold blood and just walk away like he didn't have any remorse for what he did. I don't even know who I would contact about Jerry. Does he have any family? Obviously, everyone has family, the question is whether there are people to call.

"Penny for your thoughts?" Tommy asked, holding a penny on the palm of his hand.

"I don't think one penny would be enough." I said.

"I figured." Tommy said.

"Thanks for trying." I said, looking at Tommy. "And thanks for walking with me."

"It was not a problem." Tommy said. I looked into Tommy's eyes. They shined under the moon. I could see they were a nice shade of blue. Tommy and I leaned in, but before our lips could touch I pulled away and Tommy coughed awkwardly. "So, there is a question on everyone's mind, but don't have the courage to ask. What are we going to do now?"

"I don't know." I said. "I don't know what we're going to do, but first I need to burry my friend."

"Here?" Tommy asked.

"No." I said. "Jamestown where his family is. He should be buried by his loved ones."

Two days later, everything was set. A coffin was picked out and Jerry was ready to go. So was I. Charles found someone from Jerry's family and called them to meet us after I land. None of the boys were happy with what was going on, but I wasn't letting them come with me. Derek was probably expecting me to bring all of them especially Michael, but I decided to leave them here. After a lot of begging from Tommy, I agreed to Tommy accompanying me.

No words were said as I silently said goodbye to the boys and the twins. Luckily, Charles is letting the boys stay at the house with him and the girls instead of being alone in the bed and breakfast while I'm gone. After the silent goodbye Tommy and I left in a taxi that followed the funeral car holding Jerry to the closest airport which was an hour away in a different direction then I originally came into town. The taxi ride was silent, at least in my part it was. Tommy however talked up the taxi driver the whole way there. Not that I blame him. There is only so much silence a person can take. I stayed quiet. Not that they would have paid attention if I did speak. I watched out the window as tree after tree flew by. It was sunny, the hottest it's been since we arrived, but I feel like we're standing in the downpour with nothing ahead of us except more downpour.

We arrived at the airport and after paying the taxi driver I watched as Jerry was wheeled in the direction of the luggage that goes into the airplane. Is that how people see him right now? As luggage? Tommy grabbed my hand and lead me into the airport. We didn't pack much, just a carry on with enough clothes for a few days so going through airport security was easy and didn't take that long. Now we wait to be able to board the plane. Tommy was texting on his phone the whole time. Probably to his sisters or to his dad, letting them know we made it to the airport.

"Where do you think Ethan is?" Tommy asked out of the blue. I looked up from the floor to him.

"What?" I asked.

"I'm sorry to bring him up, but Der- that guy had those people stab Jerry both Derek and Ethan disappeared." Tommy said.

"I didn't even think about that." I said.

"I was thinking we could stay an extra day or two playing detective and try to find him." Tommy said.

"I don't think so." I said to Tommy. Other people were starting to come around as they too were waiting to board the plane.

"Why not?" Tommy asked. "He's your little brother. Don't you want to help him?"

"I'm here to put a friend in the ground." I said. "Nothing more."

Tommy didn't say another word. Everything between us went silent and I watched as everyone was going through security checks and heading in the direction of their gate. An hour later, someone came across the intercom calling out that our flight was now boarding. I silently got up and grabbed my bag before heading towards the gate. I didn't even know if Tommy was following me. I handed my ticket to the flight attendant and got to my seat. A few people went by before the seat next to me was occupied. I looked to see that it was Tommy. Again, nothing was said as we waited for everyone to board the plane. I had the fight the urge to go check on Jerry. I knew there wasn't a way or a reason to go check on him. He was safe. Safe as he could be anyway. Soon, everyone had boarded, and we were just waiting for takeoff. As soon as the seatbelt sign was on and the captain declared takeoff I felt myself relax. A few hours on a plan behind kicked by some kid behind me and I watched as the plane descended to land. When the plane landed I was in no hurry to get off. I knew what was waiting for me when I got off. I'm still not ready for this.

We were the last two on the plane when Tommy took my hand and lead me off the plane carrying both our carry-on bags. We walked through security check and headed out of the airport. A taxi was already waiting for us. As we got in I watched as a funereal car drove off the airport lot, heading into town. It didn't take long for the taxi to drop us off at the hotel. Tommy fell onto the bed and let out an exhausting sigh. Soon, he was asleep. I took the opportunity to take a quick shower. When I got out I didn't feel like staying in the hotel, so I found a notepad in the room and left Tommy a note before leaving the hotel.

The sun was starting to set, making the sky look a beautiful blue and orange color. I had no idea where I was going to go. I didn't have a destination, but I ended up in a restaurant. It wasn't that crowded, so it wasn't long until I was seated in the back near a window, not that I looked out it. I didn't need to remember what's out there. A sweet waitress came and took my order. We chatted for a few before she left to tend to other tables. Soon the food came, and I ate in silence. Pretty soon I'm going to have to go meet them, Jerry's family.

"Well, I'm surprised to see you here," someone said. I looked to see Derek standing a few feet away with a few goons behind him.

"Derek." I said. "He isn't here."

"I can see that." Derek said. "I've got people looking at every motel, hotel, and abandoned house in this town."

"You can look all you want, but like I said he isn't here." I said. "I came alone."

"You left my little brother alone? Unattended?" Derek asked. He chuckled. "You really are stupid."

"Not that isn't any of your business, but he isn't alone." I said. "If you don't mind. I'm here to burry someone you killed."

"Fine. I'll let you have this one, but when he's in the ground where he belongs I'll resume my search for my brother." Derek said. He walked away and out of the restaurant. I paid and left, heading back to the hotel.

"Where were you?!" Tommy said when I walked into the room. The room was trashed. "People came in and trashed the whole place looking for something."

"Michael." I said.

"What?" Tommy asked, looking at me weirdly.

"They were looking for Michael. Derek knows we are here. He thought I brought Michael with me." I said.

"How do you know?" Tommy asked.

"He found me." I said. "He seemed pretty disappointed I didn't bring Michael with me."

"He found you?!" Tommy asked loudly. "How could he have found you?!"

"He was waiting for me to arrive." I said. "He had people follow us and when I got to the restaurant he came in. The taxi driver that dropped us off at the hotel could have told him."

"So, he knows where we are staying?" Tommy asked. He started to hurry and pack his things.

"What are you doing?" I asked.

"What does it look like?" Tommy asked. "I'm packing. We need to get out of here fast before they come back."

"No, we don't." I said. Tommy stopped what he was doing and looked at me.

"What do you mean we don't?" Tommy asked. "He found you. They came and trashed our hotel room."

"I know, but they aren't going to come back or come after us." I said. I pushed things off my bed and sat down.

"How do you know?" Tommy asked.

"Because he told me." I said, shrugging my shoulders.

"What?" Tommy asked. "What do you mean he told you?"

"At the restaurant. When I told him, I didn't bring Michael with me, that I came alone to burry Jerry. He said he'd give me this one and go back to looking for Michael after the funeral." I said.

"So, I'm…" Tommy coughed awkwardly.

"Acting crazy, I know." I said. "Now, if you don't mind I have to go meet his family and explain how he died over brunch tomorrow."

"That sounds awkward." Tommy said. "Do I need to be there for this awkward brunch?"

"No, you don't." I said. "I need to do this alone."

"Good luck." Tommy said, and he left me alone with my thoughts. The clock on the wall said it was eleven in the morning. Brunch starts in half an hour. I was fully clothed and ready to go, but I was still in the hotel room. I am nervous. How am I supposed to go tell people I don't know how their loved one died? It would be fine if it was peacefully in his sleep, but it wasn't. I took a deep breath and finally got myself off my bed and out the door. The restaurant wasn't far from the hotel, so it didn't take long to get there. I was the first to arrive which gave me time to think about what I was going to say. Shortly after getting there, people started arriving. Everything was fine. First was his close friends, but then it got hard as his kids showed up with his grandkids. My heart dropped as I watched them all introduce themselves to me and take a seat. I waited until everyone ordered to start speaking.

"Um, hello," I started. Everyone looked at me, well all the adults anyway. "My name is Nicole and I had you all come here to talk to you all about Jerry and about his untimely death."

"He died from another heart attack, didn't he?" one of his kids asked. I didn't see which one. "Did he suffer?"

"Um… no n-no he didn't suffer." I said. "But he also didn't die of another heart attack. I didn't even know he had already had one."

"He had one years ago. Wait, you're the woman he went on a road trip with," his son said.

"I am." I admitted lowly.

"Then you were with him when he died." He said, standing up in his seat.

"I was." I said.

"Is there something you're not telling us?" one of his friends asked. "You seem awfully nervous for it to be a heart attack."

"It wasn't a heart attack." I said. "He… he was stabbed."

"What do you mean he was stabbed?" his daughter asked.

"Well, Derek was the reason for the road trip." I said. "We took it to get away from him. And it wasn't just us. We, uh… had Derek's brother with us."

"You're that woman?" she asked. The look she was giving me made me feel ashamed. I looked down.

"Yes, I am." I said. "Derek found us, and he stabbed him on purpose so that I'd bring Michael here."

"Did you?" someone asked. I couldn't look up to see who.

"No, I didn't." I said. "I came alone to be here when Jerry got buried. He helped me when I needed it. I didn't want anything to happen to him and trust me I feel so bad for it. I almost didn't come because I didn't know if I could face any of you because his death is my fault and I just don't think I can face you now." I said, and I quickly got up and left as fast as I could. Quickly, walking like I couldn't get away fast enough I got back to the hotel in half the time it took to get to the restaurant. Locking the door behind me, I slid down to the floor, leaning against the door and I broke down, letting the tears fall.

Two days went by and now I'm standing in front of a mirror in a black dress. Today is the day of the funeral. Tomorrow, Tommy and I are taking the first flight out of here. Originally, we weren't leaving for another day or two, but after the brunch I needed to get out of here sooner than that. Tommy came up behind me in a tux and just took my hand. We haven't really spoken much in the last couple days well at least I haven't. Tommy pulled me out of the bathroom and out of the hotel room. A limo was outside waiting for us. We got in and it started moving, taking us to the funeral home. I wasn't ready to face anyone. I still feel like a fool and ashamed for the brunch. His family tried to get ahold of me, but I never returned any of their calls. The limo pulled up to the funereal home. The parking lot was full of cars and people were parking on the street. So many people were here for Jerry. The limo stopped at the front. He got out and opened the door for us. Tommy got out first. Knowing that if I didn't move Tommy would pull me out, I got out right behind me. People starred at us as we entered. I went all the way to the back and took a seat. People started starring and whispering to each other. Soon the funeral started and everyone turned their attention off me. I tried to pay attention, but all I could do was stare at the coffin Jerry was laying in. Before I knew it people were getting up. The funereal was over and now people were getting into a line to give their condolences to his family, all standing in a line in front of Jerry. The family was everyone from the brunch. Suddenly I felt like someone was crushing my chest. I couldn't breathe.

"Let's go outside." Tommy said. He put his hand on my back and led me outside. We walked over to the side so no one would bother us. Tommy rubbed my back and said nothing as my breathing went back to normal.

"Nicole?" someone said. Tommy and I turned around to see a postal worker standing on the sidewalk.

"Yes?" I asked. He walked up the steps and handed me an envelope before walking away. The front of the envelope had my name on it. I went to turn it over to open it when I noticed writing on the back too.

"What does it say?" Tommy asked, trying to read over my shoulder.

"Don't open it until you're alone." I read out loud.

"Let's get back to the hotel then." Tommy said. We left the funeral home. We quickly got back to the hotel, looking around every corner and holding the envelope like my life depended on it. It probably did. Once we got into the room and locked the door I ripped open the envelope. "What does it say?"

"Save me, Ethan."

CHAPTER 8

Saving Ethan

"THERE ARE SO many places he could be." Tommy said, looking at a map of the town. "How are we going to find him?"

"We get help?" I said.

"From who?" Tommy asked.

"You'll see." I said, grabbing Tommy's phone.

"Who are you calling?" Tommy asked. I ignored him and dialed a number.

"Tommy is something wrong?" Charles asked after the fifth ring.

"It's not Tommy. It's Nicole." I said.

"Oh Nicole. Is Tommy alright? Is he hurt? What is he doing?" Charles asked.

"He's fine. He's looking at a map of the town." I answered. "I need a favor without you asking any questions."

"What's the favor?" Charles asked.

"I need all of them here." I said.

"All of them?" Charles asked, sounding surprised.

"Yes, all of them." I said. "I'll explain when everyone gets here."

"Fair enough. We'll see you soon." Charles said and hung up. I handed Tommy back the phone. He didn't look very happy.

"Are you insane?!" Tommy asked loudly.

"What?" I asked, getting clothes to take a shower and get out of the dress.

"You're going to bring Michael here?" Tommy asked.

"That's the idea." I said.

"What?" Tommy asked. "You're bringing Michael here on purpose."

"Would you rather leave him alone while everyone else is here?" I asked.

"No, but what do you need everyone else for?" Tommy asked.

"You'll see." I said, heading to the bathroom to take a shower.

Everyone was here by nightfall the next day. As I hoped Charles not only brought everyone, but also extra armed security. Tommy and I checked out of our hotel room this morning and into bigger rooms that could hold everyone. No one said anything as they settled in.

"Are you going to tell me what this is all about?" Charles asked Tommy was right behind him I know wondering the same thing.

"When they are all asleep." I said gesturing to Michael, Tony, Caitlyn, and Carmen. Charles turned around to them.

"Time for bed!" Charles said more loudly then he probably intended. Everyone groaned and started walking to their rooms. I grabbed Josh when he tried to follow Tony and Michael.

"Not you. We need to talk." I said. He looked at Tony and Michael before looking back at me. He followed me back to the others. I waited until the others went to their rooms and shut the door.

"Now tell us what this is all about." Tommy said as we all sat down in the living room area together.

"What are we talking about?" Josh asked.

"I would like to know the full story myself." Charles said. "Isn't this where Michael is from?"

"We're both from here." Josh said. He looked at me. "You know Derek probably already knows he's here."

"Probably." I said. "But that's not why I asked you all here."

"Then what's so important you are risking the boys life?" Charles asked.

"Saving someone." I said. I went to my bag and pulled out the note. I handed it over to Charles. He read It and then handed it to Josh and he read it also.

"This could just be a trap." Josh said. "Derek could have sent this to get you to bring Michael here."

"I've thought of that." I said. "That's what Tony is for."

"What's Tony going to do?" Tommy asked.

"Tony can sense powers. That's how I found your sisters. I found him that way. Well, he found us." I said.

"He sensed them? How?" Tommy asked.

"This isn't the time to discuss how Tony's power works." Charles said.

"He's right." I said. "We need to get back to the plan."

"I agree." Josh said. "What are you going to have Tony do?"

"Hopefully by now he can sense the difference between the twin's powers." I said.

"So that he can try to sense Ethan's power." Josh guessed.

"And see if he's really there." I agreed.

"And if he is?" Charles asked.

"Carmen can take away his powers." I said.

"And after that?" Charles asked.

"I haven't gotten that far yet." I admitted.

"You haven't?" Charles asked. He seemed surprised. "You brought us all here without having a full plan?"

"Sort of." I said. "I was hoping one would come to me once everyone got here, but I've still got nothing on how we've going to get him out if he's there."

"So, what now?" Tommy asked. I didn't answer back. To be honest I didn't really know.

"Send me in." Michael's voice said from behind us. We turned around. Michael was standing not too far away with Tony behind him.

"What do you mean send you in?" Charles asked Michael.

"The other half of Nikki's plan." Michael said. "After Tony senses if he's in there and Carmen takes his powers away you're going to need some way to get people out of there to be able to get Ethan."

"And you think we're just going to let you do it?" I asked, walking over to Michael. "When I got here his goons tossed my hotel room because he thought I was hiding you there."

"I figured that." Michael said. "But this will work and you'll save your brother."

"You think that I'd want to risk for someone else's?" I asked. "Even if he's my brother."

"He's not going to touch me." Michael said. "You're forgetting I can throw him with just one thought." I rolled my eyes. "Just trust me."

"I don't like this." I said as we all stood in the forest around the house I found Michael in. I was standing off the side with Charles, Tommy, and Josh. Tony, Michael, Carmen, and Caitlyn were a little away talking to each other. "I don't like this one bit."

"Everyone knows you don't, but you argued with him for more than three hours and he wouldn't budge." Charles said. "It's time to just accept it."

"So, I'm just supposed to stand here and let him offer himself up as bait?" I asked. I felt something cold on my wrist. I looked to see a handcuff attached to me. I watched as Tommy attached the other cuff to his wrist. "What are you doing?"

"Doing what I was asked to do and keeping you here." Tommy said.

"You think handcuffing me to you is going to stop me from stopping me?" I asked. He said nothing. I took a safety pin I had in my pocket and bent it until it was straight and then I put it in the key hole on the handcuff attached to me. I moved the pin around until the handcuff came undone. I knew it would have come in handy eventually.

"I did not see that coming." Tommy said, holding up the handcuff still attached to him.

"They are ready." Charles said.

"Oh no they aren't." I said. I was about to stop them when I flew back into the van we rented and it shut and locked without me or anyone touching it. "MICHAEL!" I shouted, banging on the door and window while trying to open it.

"I'm sorry." Michael said. He looked at me for a long moment before following Tony and the girls towards the house. As soon as they were out of sight, the doors unlocked and opened. I quickly got out and made my way back to Tommy and Charles. I would have went into the house to go after them, but the second I tried to Tommy grabbed my and held onto me tightly, not letting me move.

Seconds went by and then minutes. No noise. No sound. Nothing at all. We all stood there in silence, waiting for something to happen, but there was nothing. I started biting my lip. Shouldn't we be hearing people screaming by now? I would take a laugh at this point instead of silence.

"Someone's coming out!" Charles said. I looked in the direction Charles started pointing in. Coming out the front door was Tony and Carmen. They were coming out the door with someone between them, hanging on their shoulders. I knew that it wasn't Michael because the person was too short to be Michael. As they came close I realized it was Ethan. They got to us and they all fell to the ground, Ethan landing flat onto his back. He looked bad, like they used him for some target practice. Josh hurried over with the first aid kit.

"Where's Caitlyn?" Charles asked. I looked around and realized Caitlyn wasn't with us. Neither was Michael.

"Michael hasn't come out either." I said. I looked at Tony and Carmen. They looked down, not looking at anyone. "Tell us what happened."

"Well, the plan we had worked fine. At first." Tony said. "I sensed Ethan and we found him like this in a room upstairs. Then Michael and I realized it was way too quiet around here and way too easy to get upstairs. It was a trap. He knew we were coming and he knew exactly what we were planning."

"He knew we were coming?" I asked. They nodded. "But how?"

"He said an old friend told him." Carmen said.

"Old friend?" I asked, confused. "But the only old friend of his that knew what the plan was…" I stopped talking and turned to Josh. He was looking at me, but they weren't apology eyes or even sad looking. He was smirking. He stood up.

"Sorry Nicole." Josh said. "It was really nice playing this game with you, but Derek always wins."

"Why?" I asked. "After everything he did to you. After everything I did for you. How could you go to him? How could you sell us out like that?"

"He is my best friend. He will always be my best friend." Josh said. "What did you expect me to do?"

"What's going on?" Tommy asked, but I ignored him. I couldn't take my eyes off Josh.

"You betrayed us. Now he's got Michael and Caitlyn." I said.

"Michael was on purpose and after I told him what the girl can do… well it was quite obvious we need her too." Josh said.

"Everyone get in the van. Everyone, but you." I said, pointing to Josh. "You can go back to your best friend and tell him I'll be back for Michael and Caitlyn."

Switching hotels wasn't easy. With Josh having an alliance with Derek I couldn't trust any of the hotels in Jamestown so we had to find one in a city over. There was some convention one of the hotels so we could easily blend in at the hotel. Putting a 'do not disturb' sign on our hotel door so that no one disturbed Ethan who was still recovering we all left the hotel, heading to Jamestown. We weren't going to attempt to get them back much to Charles' dismay, but we don't know who he's got surrounding them or how many. We could easily be going into another trap to get Tony and Carmen to use their powers. So today we are observing. We parked outside the hotel we were at when Josh portrayed us and got out to walk around.

"Isn't being out in the open a bit dangerous?" Charles asked.

"Yes and no." I said. "He isn't going to attack us when he's got Michael back."

"So, we're safe?" Tommy asked, looking everywhere as we walked.

"For now." I said. "Soon we will get them back and then we won't be safe."

"We are going to get them back?" Charles asked.

"Of course." I said. "This is just an intel mission."

Two hours of walking around and everyone was tired. Carmen complained enough times to drive everyone crazy. Enough walking to make everyone hungry so we decided to stop at a diner. Not many people were in here so being seated wasn't an issue. Once we were seated and ordered drinks and food I started to relax, but that didn't last long. Coming into the diner and sitting in the corner by the window was two of Derek's goons. I wouldn't be worried and just think they were sent in to scare everyone, expect they've been following us since we started walking. I tried to ignore them and get into the conversation with the others, but I just couldn't. The food came and everyone started eating. I decided to let the goons sitting there go and just enjoy my food. It was going well and I was starting to enjoy myself until they stood up and walked over. They stood next to our table. Everyone stopped eating and looked at them. No one said anything to anyone. One of the goons pulled a note out of his pocket and set it on the table in front of me before they both walked out of the diner together. I took the note and opened it. It had an address on it and I knew that address. Tony and I have both been there before.

It was Jerry's address. They were at Jerry's house.

I stood up, set money on the table, and left the diner. I wasn't going after the goons, but I knew where I was heading. I could hear everyone behind me, but I knew that if I stopped either I would talk myself out of whatever it is I'm doing or they would and I cannot do that. They were telling me to stop or slow down, but I just couldn't do it. The house was close. I was starting to see the roof come into view. I started walking faster the more the house came into view. Before I could reach the front yard, I was grabbed from behind.

"You are insane!" Tommy said as he turned me around. Tony, Carmen, and Charles were right behind him. Everyone was out of breath. "What do you think you're doing?"

"Going in there." I said. I tried to turn back around, but Tommy wouldn't let me. "Would you mind letting me go?"

"No, I will not." Tommy said. "Not until you no longer want to go in there."

"It's Jerry's house." I said.

"But those were Derek's goons that gave you the note with the address on it." Tony pointed out.

"I know who gave me the note." I said. "But it's Jerry's house."

"I know and I understand why you want to go, but it could easily just be a trap." Tommy said.

"Don't you think I know it could be a trap or that it probably is one." I said.

"Then why are you going?" Tommy asked. "If you know this is a trap then why are you going to go run right in?"

"Because that is Jerry's house he is taking over so I need to." I said. "Now if you don't mind I've got someplace to be."

I yanked myself out to Tommy's arms and walked across the yard. No noise could be heard from outside or inside. I walked up the steps onto the porch. Slowly, I walked to the front door. Part of me hoped the door was locked, but I knew I didn't have any luck in this situation. I turned the door knob and slowly opened the door, walking inside. It was dark. There was still no noise or movements as I walked more into the house. I got to the doorway leading into a different room when the front door slammed shut and something hit me hard. I saw someone stand in front of me before darkness took over and I passed out.

CHAPTER 9

Captured

COLD WATER WAS splashed on my face. I coughed and spit the water out before I opened my eyes. My head lifted up and I had to adjust my eyes to the sudden light. Once again my hands were tired. This time they were tired above me and I was hanging from whatever I was tied to.

"Nice to see you awake Nicole." I heard Derek say as he came into the room.

"Where are they?" I asked immediately.

"You mean your little friends that tried to stop you from entering the house?" Derek asked. I didn't answer. "They are upstairs with my men watching them."

"Like they watched me the last time you had me?" I asked. Derek smirked, but didn't say anything. "Where's Michael? Where is Caitlyn?"

"Don't worry about them." Derek said. He walked over to the other side where there was bottles of liquor on a stand.

"Don't touch that! It doesn't belong to you!" I shouted, trying to move around and get free.

"Well, if Jerry wants me to leave his stuff alone he can come and tell me himself." Derek said laughing. There was no noise coming from anywhere in the house." I watched as Derek poured himself a drink.

"wait until I get free." I said, giving Derek a dirty look.

"What are you going to do?" Derek asked. "I've got guns and men that will gladly shoot you. You have nothing." Derek walked out of the room without another word, turning off the light as he left.

It was awhile before someone came back in the room. It was completely dark so I couldn't see them, but I could hear their footsteps. They didn't come towards me. Instead they went to the other side of the room. I had no idea what they were doing and that terrified me.

"He plans on killing you. I hope you know that," a voice said. I'm guessing it belongs to the person who entered the room. "You and all your friends." It was a girl's voice.

"Who are you?" I asked into the darkness. There was a chuckle.

"Me? My name is Lexi," the voice said.

"Lexi," I said. "Can you tell me how you know that?"

"I read it in his mind." Lexi said. "I read everything he plans on doing to you and all your friends."

"That's crazy. People can't read minds." I said.

"Right." Lexi said. "Just like how Michael can't move things with his mind. Your brother can't feel the emotions and pain of everyone around him. Carmen can't take away someone's powers. And Caitlyn can't copy someone's power. Or how Tony can't feel when someone's power is near."

"Sense." I said.

"What?' Lexi asked.

"It's not feeling when someone with powers is near." I said. "It's sensing."

"Are you admitting they have powers?" Lexi asked.

"No, I'm not admitting anything." I said. "I'm just simply correcting you."

"Right." Lexi said.

"How did Derek find you?" I asked.

"He has his resources." Lexi said. "After you took Michael he sent his men to find someone that could help him get Michael back for good and I guess I'm that someone."

"Where were you when he found you?" I asked.

"I was a college student happily living my life at NYU." Lexi said. "Before you even think it I have never used my powers for personal gain. I got into NYU by working my ass off and earning my spot there."

"I wasn't going to think that or even say that." I said. There was no noise coming from anywhere in the room. I thought Lexi left the room, but then I heard movements of someone coming towards me."

"He was wrong." Lexi said.

"Who?" I asked. By this time my arms have gone completely numb, but I need to know what she knows.

"Derek. He said you wanted to destroy Michael and he wanted me to use my power to see how you were going to do it." Lexi said. "But reading your mind, you aren't looking to destroy Michael. You want to help him."

"Someone is trying to destroy him, but it's not me. It's the person who brought you here." I said.

"Derek?" Lexi asked. "That explains why he is always careful about what he thinks when I'm around."

"What about his goons?" I asked.

"His what?" Lexi asked.

"His men with guns." I said. "I call them his goons. They act like it."

"They don't know much. I think he's keeping most of them in the dark. They mainly just do what he says because they are afraid he's going to kill them if they don't." Lexi said.

"Is Derek here?" I asked.

"No, it's just you, me, and your friends that are locked upstairs." Lexi said. "They are all thinking about you especially the one I've heard people call Tommy."

"What do you mean?" I asked. "I met him a few days ago."

"So? Don't you know you can fall in love with someone in just a matter of seconds?" Lexi asked.

"What are you talking about?" I asked. Lexi didn't answer me. She just chuckled as I heard a car pull up.

"Derek is back with Michael and Caitlyn." Lexi said. "You do realize Derek only captured her because she can copy Michael's power, right?"

"I know. You better get out of here before he finds you in here." I said. Without another word Lexi left the room, just in time for Derek to walk in. He flipped a switch on and the light shined throughout the entire room blinding me.

"NICOLE!" I heard Michael shout and run towards me. He put my face in his hands.

"Hey, how's it hanging?" I joked. "Get it... hanging." He rolled his eyes at my joke and looked back at Derek.

"Why did you do this to her?" Michael asked. I felt the roped bonding me loosen and I fell to the ground. I rubbed my wrists where the ropes were tied.

"Thanks for that." I told Michael.

"I didn't say you could untie her." Derek said to Michael. "Go get her friends." Derek told some of his goons. They nodded and left the room.

"The others?" Michael asked, looking at me. "They're here too?"

"They followed me." I said. Michael looked at Derek as I heard people being shoved towards the room. A second later Tony, Charles, Tommy, and Carmen were shoved into the room.

"Caitlyn!" Carmen and Charles shouted. Carmen ran to Caitlyn who hugged her sister tight. I could tell the goons were trying to get in between them to separate them, but something was holding them back so they couldn't. It was Michael holding them back.

"We're missing someone." Derek said, looking around at everyone. "Tell Lexi she is needed and bring our other friend from his room."

"Sir we can't-" the goon Derek was talking to tried to say as he tried to move.

"Michael let them go. They aren't going to touch anyone." Derek said, but they still couldn't move.

"Michael, it's alright." I said, touching his arm. He let them go and the goons left.

"Sure, you he listens to." Derek said, rolling his eyes.

"He trusts me." I said.

"For now." Derek said.

Everything went silent as we waited for people to come into the room. I would finally see a face to the voice that was just talking to me. I started getting feeling back in my arms, but they started getting sore. I shouldn't be surprised since I was strung up by rope. I looked around the room. Tommy and Tony were by the doorway they came into like they didn't know what to do or where to go. Derek sat himself on the couch with some of the goons standing around him waiting for Derek to tell them to do something. Michael was still by my side with Caitlyn, Carmen, and Charles standing together in a little hurdle. Noises came from somewhere in the house. Lexi came into the room first and sat in one of the arm chairs in Jerry's living room. The next person that got shoved in by a goon surprised me.

Josh.

It was Josh, but he looked badly beaten. He looked practically unrecognizable. He had cuts all over his arms, no doubt also around the rest of his body. He looked around the room with the one eye that wasn't swollen. I couldn't tell if he was shocked to see us or not.

"Traitor!" Tony shouted at Josh. He started walking towards Josh, his hands in a tight fist. He was ready to fight him and I knew it.

"Tommy, stop him!" I shouted since he was the one closest. Moving quickly, Tommy wrapped his arms around Tony. Tony struggled to get from Tommy's grip.

"LET ME GO! HE IS NOTHING BUT A TRAITOR! HE DESERVES TO BE BEATEN!" Tony shouted.

"Not until you calm down." Tommy said as Tony still struggled.

"Why should I? He deserves someone to kick his ass!" Tony said.

"Looks to me like he already got it." Tommy said. Tony looked over at Josh. Josh couldn't even look at anyone. He just kept his head down.

"He should have known he was being tricked. He read enough the last eight years, you'd think he would have been smart." Derek said.

"Can we get this over with? I have plans tonight with a very cute bartender and I don't plan on being late." Lexi said.

"Michael, you remember Lexi, don't you?" Derek asked.

"Yes. What is she doing here?" Michael asked.

"For those of you that don't know, Lexi has the power to read minds." Derek said. "I asked her to join us to take a peek into someone's mind."

Derek looked at me.

"You're going to use Lexi to get your brother to turn against me and be back on your side." I said, remembering what Lexi told me.

"I only want him to see the truth and Lexi here will help me do just that." Derek said. Derek pulled me away and made me sit across from Lexi. "Now, I'm going to ask you questions that I know you're going to lie to me so my new best friend is going to tell everyone what you are really thinking."

"Or for you to fake all the answers." Tommy said.

"I'm not doing that." Derek said. "Lexi is telling me what she thinks when she answers."

"And we're supposed to trust you?" Tommy asked.

"Yes, you are." Derek said. "Why wouldn't you?"

"I can think of a few reasons." I said.

"Let's just get this over with." Derek said. Everyone stayed quiet. "What's the real reason you're helping Mikey?"

"To help him with his powers." I said. Derek looked at Lexi.

"She's thinking about using his powers." Lexi said. "She wants to use him for something big."

"That's a lie!" Michael said. "She's done nothing but help me."

"What are your plans after you get what you want?" Derek asked like Michael didn't just say anything.

"I don't have any plans." I said. Derek looked at Lexi.

"She plans on getting rid of everyone permanently." Lexi said. Lexi stood up. At first I thought she was going to do something to me or one of us, but instead she looked at Derek.

"I CAN'T DO IT!" Lexi shouted. "YOU ARE AN EVIL GUY!" Lexi shouted at Derek.

"What's going on?" Charles asked.

"He made me do it!" Lexi said, covering her face in her hands. "He lied to me."

"Lied about what?" I asked.

"I didn't lie about anything." Derek said.

"He said when he brought me here that you were evil. He said you wanted to kill his brother and he needed my help to uncover the truth, but when you all came he gave me a list of answers and told me that if I didn't trade your answers with the ones he gave me then he'd kill me." Lexi said. Tears were starting to fall down her cheeks.

"You little bitch!" Derek said. He tried lunging at Lexi, but I got in front of her. He never reached us. Before he could, he was thrown across the room without anyone touching him. I looked back at Michael, but he wasn't looking at me or Derek. He was looking at Caitlyn. Caitlyn was the one looking at Derek like he was something to kill.

"Let him go." Michael said, touching Caitlyn's arm. She looked at him. "Trust me. He's not worth it." Caitlyn looked at Michael for another long moment before Derek fell to the floor.

"Let's get out of here." I said, taking Lexi's hand. "All of us."

CHAPTER 10

Separate Ways

W E LEFT IN a hurry. We grabbed the barely conscious Ethan from the hotel and we left without another glance back. Lexi wanted to go back to her life at NYU but considering she portrayed Derek he'll be looking for her now and that will probably be the first place he'll look for her. She didn't agree with it, but she stayed with us. For now.

We drove together in the van, Tommy, Charles, and I taking turns driving. One drive as far as they could while the other two slept. We made it to Utah before the van finally died beyond repair. We got a hotel room and took turns showering.

"Do I need to get us a new van?" Charles asked as I came out of the bathroom, feeling refreshed after my shower.

"No, I think we should go in two cars." I said. "It was be less suspicious instead of seeing a giant van full of people."

"Are we all staying together?" Tommy asked. I thought about it for a moment.

"No." I said. Everyone stopped what they were doing and looked at me.

"We're not staying together?" Michael asked. He looked over at Caitlyn. I sighed.

"No." I repeated. "I think that for now we should get two cars and separate into two groups. One going in one direction and the other going into a different direction. Just a bit until things with Derek calms down and then we'll meet up again."

"What if they don't calm down?" Josh asked.

"But who goes with who?" Charles asked, ignoring Josh. Everyone has been ignoring Josh.

"I haven't figured that out yet." I said which was true, I haven't. There are more people than when I started. I need to keep Michael with me, but now there is also Ethan and Lexi. Of course, Josh and Tony need to stay separated since they have been going at it every chance they get since we left.

"I don't want to apart from my girls." Charles said.

"Of course, you can't." I agreed.

"I want to go with you." Tommy said, looking at me.

"Really?" My voice sounded more excited then I intended, making everyone chuckle and my face turn a nice shade of red. Lexi was giving me a I told you so look from across the room where she was sitting with the girls.

"So how do we decided who goes with who?" Lexi asked. "Do we draw straws? Pick numbers?"

"No, none of that." I said. "Josh will go with Charles and Tommy will go with me."

"That settles where you normal people will go." Michael said. "But what about the rest of us?"

"Well, Tony and Josh can barely be in a room together for five minutes without a fight breaking out between the two so Tony will come with Tommy, Michael, and I." I said.

"So, I am going with you." Michael said.

"You're the one Derek wants." I pointed out.

"We'll go with our dad, right?" Carmen and Caitlyn asked.

"Of course, you will go with your dad." I said. I turned to Lexi and Ethan. "Which leaves you two."

"What about us?" Ethan asked.

"Well, if you're with me it would give Derek something to hold over me if he finds us so I'll send you with Charles." I said. I turned to Lexi. "As for you Lexi, I need you for two reasons. One you can read minds so you'll be able to know if Derek or one of his goons are near."

"And what's the other reason?" Lexi asked.

"I know you want to back to your life at NYU, but I also know that I can't happen until this whole Derek situation is dealt with once in for all. So, for the time being you are sticking with me so I know you don't sneak off." Lexi huffed and stormed off.

Charles bought two different cars. A nice black care for him and everyone going with him. After telling him it's best if I don't know where he is going, Charles and his group left first. Tommy got a red car, but we stayed another night to make sure the others get a head start. I didn't really have a final destination as Tommy and I packed the car up with everyone's things and food for the road trip.

"Let's go!" Tommy shouted when everything was all set. Michael and Tony came out and got into the back seat. "Where's Lexi?"

"She says she's not coming." Michael said through the window. I sighed.

"Get in the car I'll get her." Tommy nodded and got in the driver's seat as I walked back into the room. "Come on bus is leaving."

"I'm not going." Lexi said. She was scrolling through something on a phone.

"Where did you get a phone?" I asked.

"I swiped it from Tommy's pocket." Lexi said. "All my friends are wondering where I am. Can't I message them to let them know I'm alright?"

"No, you can't." I said. She sighed. "Listen Lexi I know it's hard, but once this is all done you can go back and everything will be normal."

"Hate to break it to you, but I have never been normal all my life." Lexi said. I chuckled.

"Fine. As normal as you can be now let's go." I said. "All the men are waiting."

As we left the hotel room, taking one last look around the room making sure we don't miss anything Lexi handed me back Tommy's phone. I handed it back to Tommy without a word as Lexi got in the car and we were off.

A few days later we were driving through Nevada. I was driving while everyone else slept. Tommy and I have been taking turns driving while the other three complain about being in the back seat. Tommy has talked to Charles twice since we left, never letting him tell him us where they are, but according to Tommy they sound like they are surrounded by people and seem to be enjoying themselves. I feel terrible for splitting up a family.

"They don't blame you." Lexi said from behind me. "None of them blame you from making them go separate ways."

"How do you know?" I asked.

"I read minds remember." Lexi said, chuckling. "When's the last time you got sleep?"

"Well, I took over driving at eight in the morning and it's now three in the morning." I said, looking at the clock on the dashboard.

"Pull over." Lexi said. I looked in the mirror confused. "Come on pull over." Too tired to argue I did as she said and pulled over to the side of the road. Everyone else woke up.

"What's going on?" asked a groggy Tommy.

"Nicole has been driving for almost twenty hours and you drove twenty-four hours before that. We haven't stopped anywhere so you two can get proper sleep so I'm going to drive for a while so you both can sleep." Lexi said. She got out of the car and opened my door making me almost fall out of the car. I got out and into her seat next to Michael. I put my head on Michael's shoulder and instantly fell asleep.

I woke up to the sun beaming down on my face. I was in the car, but I was the only one in the car. I quickly got out of the car there was no way Derek found us, right? We were parked at a beach. I could see Lexi sitting in the sand a few feet away. I started walking towards her.

"He didn't find us." Lexi said as I sat down next to her. "The guys saw the water and we all decided to have some fun."

"How come no one woke me? What if I wanted to have some fun too?" I asked. "Where are the guys?"

"Tony and Michael are in the water and Tommy went to get food and then he was going to wake you up to eat." Lexi said.

"Want to play a joke on Tommy?" I asked, looking for any signs of him.

"What did you have in mind?" Lexi asked.

"Well, I'm going to go hide and when Tommy comes to get me to eat pretend like you don't know where I went." I said.

"Oh, he's going to throw a fit." Lexi said. "Let's do it."

I smiled and took off, making sure Michael and Tony aren't noticing me. I found a nice spot to hide where none of them could see me, but I could still see them. Ten minutes into hiding Tommy came into view. He was carrying a lot of food. He set it down next to Lexi. He took in the direction of the car as Lexi called the boys over. They came out of the water and sat down and Tommy came running over. I watched as he was talking fast to the boys and Lexi. Soon the boys were all freaking out as Lexi stood there, trying not to laugh. After twenty minutes of watching them all I decided to make where I was hiding.

"Hey guys." I said when I got close enough. All three of them turned and looked at me.

"NICOLE!" Tommy, Michael, and Tony said in unison.

"Where were you?" Tommy asked. "I went to get you to eat and you weren't there."

"I know. I woke up alone in a car." I said, crossing my arms. "So, think about you three just felt and know how I felt waking up alone in a car."

"You looked tired so I decided to just let you sleep." Tommy said.

No one said anything. We just sat around in the sand watching the waves move in as we ate. My mind wondered to the others. I'm starting to regret this decision to separate from the others. I know why we did this to protect each other, but what if we could protect each other better if we were together? I separated Tommy from his father and sisters. And I had them take Ethan who I haven't seen most of his life and shouldn't have sent away.

"I need to make a phone call." I said as I got up and walked away. I pulled out the phone Tommy had gotten that was a nonretractable and dialed a phone number.

"Tommy?" Charles asked when he answered.

"No, it's Nicole." I said.

"Nicole? Is there something wrong? Is Tommy alright?" Charles asked.

"He's alright. Everyone is fine." I said.

"Then why did you call?" Charles asked. "Not that it's not nice to hear from you, but wasn't there a point to going our separate ways?"

"That's why I am calling." I said.

"What do you mean?" Charles asked. I could hear some people in the background and Charles shushing them.

"I mean that this idea of going separate ways is stupid. I separated you from your son. I separated myself from my only brother who I haven't seen since he was four." I said.

"What are you getting at Nicole?" Charles asked.

"I want you all to come back and join us." I said.

"ARE YOU CRAZY?!" I heard Tommy shout behind me. I turned around to see Tommy, Lexi, and the boys standing behind me.

"I'll call you back." I told Charles and hung up before he could say anything. "What are you guys doing? Spying on me?"

"Better question is what are you doing?" Tommy asked in a nasty tone.

"Making a phone call before I was rudely interrupted." I said.

"A phone call to my dad." Tommy said.

"Hey buddy who I call is my business." I said.

"You're making a big mistake." Tommy said.

"No, the mistake was separating everyone." I said. They all looked at each other before looking back at me. "At the time I thought us going our separate ways would be a good thing. You know that maybe if we went our separate ways then Derek wouldn't be able to figure who has Michael and that maybe just maybe he'd give up, but now I'm starting to realize how stupid that all is."

"So, what are you saying?" Lexi asked.

"I'm saying it's time the others came to us." I said, getting ready to dial Charles number again.

"Do what you think you need to do, but I don't like this." Tommy said and he walked away.

"For the record I don't like this either." Michael said, following Tommy. I looked at Tony and Lexi. They didn't say anything to me. They just stared at me. I hit the call button and listened as the phone rang a few times before someone answered.

"Nicole, is everything alright? You hung up rather quickly." Charles said.

"Yes, everything is fine." I lied. Lexi gave me a look before walking away. I wonder if it's for what I'm about to do or because I'm lying about it.

"What were you saying before you hung up?" Charles asked. "Something about a mistake?"

"I want you to come join us. No questions just come join us. I'll text you our location." I said and hung up before he could say anything like disagree. I sent the location of where we were before throwing the phone on the ground and smashing it with my foot. Even if it was nonretractable I wasn't taking the chance.

Three days later, a knock on the hotel room door showed that everyone else had finally arrived. Tommy silently answered the door, letting Charles and Josh walk through.

"The girls are on their way up." Charles said.

"What about Ethan?" I asked. Charles and Josh exchanged looks.

"Nicole, Ethan left." Charles said, sighing.

"What do you mean he left?" I asked.

"We stopped at a rest stop on the way here and he told us he was leaving." Josh said.

"And no one stopped him?" I asked.

"We tried." Charles said. He coughed awkwardly. "He... uh... he said he hasn't needed you before he doesn't need or want you now. I'm sorry."

"TOMMY!" the twins shouted in unison as they came into the room. They both jumped on him at the same time as they were little kids, making him fall to the ground.

"Hi to you girls too." Tommy said laughing.

"We missed you." Caitlyn said.

"I missed you girls too." Tommy said. "But I didn't want you girls back here. I didn't want any of you back here."

"I figured you were the reason she hung up on me the first time, but she called us first." Charles said. "Truth is we were going to call within the next few days if you didn't to see if you would join us or we'd join you. It just didn't feel right to be so separated from you or anyone."

"You were?" I asked. Tommy gave me a look like he was telling me not to agree.

"We were in Florida missing everyone. Josh was even missing Tony even though they've done nothing but argue since we rescued Josh." Charles said. Josh and Tony looked at each other before looking away again. "A few more days and I would have been making the call myself."

"But dad-" Tommy started to say, but Charles cut him off.

"We are better together." Charles said. "We are all better together."

The room fell silent. No one said anything. We didn't need to. Charles words were true. We are all better together. I was about to show the girls their room thinking they'd want to get cleaned up from the drive here from Florida when something on the television caught my attention. It was a picture of Lexi with a caption below it.

"NYU student kidnapped."

CHAPTER 11

Kidnapped

I LOOKED AT EVERYONE. The expressions on their face must have matched mine. Confusion. Her photo was still on the television and then woman so I turned the television up.

"A student at NYU by the name of Lexi Livingston has been reported missing and has not been seen in weeks. She was reported last seen visiting family in Jamestown, New York, but was taken from there by a group of people and has not been heard from since. If anyone has seen Lexi or knows her whereabouts please dial the number you see at the bottom of your screen," the news woman said and then went to another piece of news. Everyone looked over at Lexi.

"I was not kidnapped." Lexi said.

"We know that." I said. "But the world doesn't."

"Do you even have any family in Jamestown?" Charles asked. "She said you were last seen visiting family in Jamestown, New York."

"I don't have any family in Jamestown though." Lexi said. "I don't even know anyone in Jamestown. Who does?"

"I do." Michael said. "And you all have met him."

"Derek." I said, realizing when Jamestown was so familiar. How could I even forget? I looked at Lexi. "He doesn't know where we are so he's trying to draw us out by exposing that we have you."

"What's going to happen?" Lexi asked. "What if they find us or Derek does?"

"Well, if they find us everyone eighteen and over will go to jail for kidnapping and those less than eighteen will go somewhere else. And if Derek finds us we could end up taken by Derek or worse... we could end up dead."

"Dead?" Charles asked. "What do you mean we could end up dead?"

"I don't know." I said. "I'm just saying it's a possibility that if he did find us he could take us or kill us."

"I don't want anyone to die for me." Lexi said.

"No one is dying for anyone." I said.

"Maybe the girls and I should go so they don't get hurt." Charles said. Everyone started talking all at once.

"Everyone hold up." I said, but no one was listening. They were still all talking to each other at once. "HEY! HOLD UP!" Everyone went silent. "No one needs to go anywhere and no one is dying for anyone."

"Then what do you expect us to do?" Tony asked.

"Stay low for a while. We obviously can't stay in hotels because Lexi can easily be spotted by housekeepers so let's rent a place big enough for everyone." I said. Everyone talked at once again, but eventually agreed.

A week later, Charles and I found a place big enough for everyone. Lexi hasn't left the hotel room since her face has been on the news. She's been afraid she is going to be spotted by someone. Every time she needed something she sent one of the guys to get it. Today we were getting ready to move into the house. Everyone, but Lexi. Lexi wasn't moving or even packing her clothes.

"What if someone recognizes me?" Lexi asked. "What if we're moving and one person recognizes me from the news. That's all it's going to take. Just one person and it could all go wrong."

"That is not going to happen." I said. "We'll put a disguise on you so no one will."

"But-" Lexi said, but I interrupted her.

"But nothing." I said. Lexi opened her mouth to say something but closed it. "Let's go!" I shouted at everyone. One by one everyone took their things and left the hotel room until it was like just Lexi and I in the room. I put a scarf over to head and handed her some sunglasses before making her leave the hotel room.

It took an hour to drive to the new house. The whole ride everyone was looking nervous. We got to the house and we pulled into a gate. Charles put a code into the gate keypad. The gate opened and Charles pulled through the driveway. The house came into view. It was huge and brick. It looked like a house built in the fifties.

"Wow, this looks amazing." Caitlyn said. Charles parked the car and everyone got out.

"Some of you will have to share a room, but there is plenty of room for everyone." Charles said.

"Just minus the servants." Tommy said.

"Yes, minus the servants." I said. "But the good thing is the gate only opens for a code that only Charles and I know."

"We don't get to know the code?" Tommy asked.

"No." Charles said. "We think it's in the best interest for everyone if the code stays just between Nicole and I?"

"What if we want to leave? How would we get back in?" Michael asked.

"Someone will always be home and there is a call button on the box so hit the button and someone will always be able to buzz you in." I said. "Let's unload and unpack."

Everything we had was unpacked and furniture was brought in so it actual house for everyone. The news was still playing the story that Lexi was reported missing, but so far no one has reported any updates about it. No one is close to finding her not that she is actually missing. Only Charles and I knowing the code was a good idea at the time, but by now I'm not so sure. All of them have been coming and going so much that if it wasn't for their safety I would have taken the gate down.

"Who is it?" I asked as someone hit the buzzer to come in.

"It's Tony." He said through the speaker. I rolled my eyes and hit the button to let him in before heading back to the living room where Charles was waiting.

"Who was it?" Charles asked.

"Tony this time." I said. "The others will be coming soon."

"Should we just give them the code instead of having to let them in all the time. The only one who stays inside is Lexi." Charles said.

"She wouldn't be inside all the time if it wasn't for the news story." I pointed out.

"Derek ruins everything." Charles said.

"Speaking of Derek," a voice that wasn't Tony's said behind us. We jumped up and turned around.

"Derek." I said. He was standing in the doorway with a gun pointed at Tony. "How did you find us?"

"Well, I guess Lexi got tired of having her face on the news." Derek said as Lexi was brought down by goons.

"I'm sorry Nicole." Lexi looked ashamed.

"Shut up!" the goon behind her said.

"Make me." Lexi said. The goon was about to do something when he flew backwards. Michael came into view.

"I saw the gate was open and I knew something was wrong." Michael said. "What are you doing here Derek?"

"What? No, hello for your loveable brother?" Derek asked.

"You're not loveable." I said.

"I think I am." Derek said. "Now that's get down to business." Derek looked at Michael.

"What are you doing here?" Michael asked.

"Without you and your freakish power no one will give me the money they owe me so I'm going to need you to come home and go back to work for me and get me my money from people that owe me money." Derek said.

"No." Michael said.

"What?" Derek asked. "What did you just say to me?"

"I said no." Michael said. "I'm not going back with you and I definitely not be going back to work for you."

"Oh, I think you will." Derek said.

"Give me one good reason." Michael said. Derek smirked and looked at me.

"Turn on the news." Derek said. No one moved and said anything. "Go ahead and turn it on." I turned around a grabbed the television remote that was near me. I turned on the television and flipped to a news channel since that seems to be where he was going when he said to turn it on. The picture of Lexi was on the screen.

"You wanted to show us the same story you started that's been playing for weeks?" Tommy asked. I turned around at his voice. I didn't realize he was back. It looked like everyone was now back.

"Just watch and listen." Derek said. I went back to the television and turned the volume up.

"Lexi Livingston has been missing for weeks and there have been no leads on finding her until now. We've got reports that someone has called into the tip line saying that they know who took Lexi. Police are issuing a warrant for the arrest of Nicole Sullivan. Nicole is described as a Caucasian woman in her mid-twenties with long blonde hair and blue eyes. She was last seen traveling with a group of people. If anyone knows her whereabouts or has seen her you are to contact the number at the bottom of your screen," a news anchor said. Everyone looked from the television to me, then to Derek, and then back to me. I could just stare at Derek. Michael spoke first.

"Derek, what did you do?" Michael asked.

"I just did my duty as a citizen." Derek said.

"You lied to the police to get them after Nicole." Tommy said. Tommy tried to advance on Derek, but his goons came forward and pointed their guns making Tommy back off.

"No, I didn't." Derek said. "Lexi was last seen leaving with you all and technically Nicole is your little ring leader so it would be her that they would go after."

"He's right." I said.

"What?!" Everyone said in unison.

"Think about it. None of you would be here if it wasn't for me. None of us would know each other. We wouldn't be in this big house with guns pointed at us while being stalked by a power crazed moron." I said.

"Exactly." Derek said. Everyone snickered at Derek for not noticing I called him a power crazed moron. "So, here is how it's going to go. Michael is going to come with us and no one is going to try anything or come after us. We will be left alone."

"We both know I'm going to come for him and take him back so what is the point in doing this?" I asked.

"Oh, I don't think you will. Not this time." Derek said, smirking.

"And what makes you think that?" I asked.

"Because if you do I'll call that number that was at the bottom of the screen and let it slip of your exact location." Derek said as he smirked at me.

"You wouldn't." I challenged.

"Oh, I would." Derek said. He turned to Michael. "Let's go Michael. We don't need these people."

"Nicole," Michael said, looking at me.

"Go." I said. Michael looked at me for a moment before walking out with Derek. Everyone just stared at me as they left. I walked away from everyone, wanting to be alone.

Weeks have gone by since Derek took Michael back. We were all still in the same house. I kept my word and stayed put. No one showed up for me or Lexi which means Derek didn't call the police either. No one has said a word to me since Michael left either, but I don't blame them. I let Michael leave and every time they try to come up with a plan to go save him I shut the plan down.

I walked into the living room and everyone went silent at once. They were planning again.

"What is the plan this time?" I asked.

"What plan?" Charles asked.

"Your next plan to go after Michael." I said. "You might as well tell me so I can turn it down."

"AT LEAST WE'RE TRYING TO DO SOMETHING TO HELP HIM UNLIKE YOU!" Josh shouted, standing up. "HOW COULD YOU JUST STAND THERE AND LET HIM LEAVE WITH THAT DICK?! YOU KNOW WHAT KIND OF GUY HE IS! YOU KNOW WHAT HE IS CAPABLE OF! YOU KNOW WHAT HE COULD DO TO MICHAEL! MICHAEL IS PROBABLY DEAD RIGHT NOW AND YOU DON'T EVEN CARE!"

"He's not." I said calmly.

"What?" Josh asked.

"He isn't dead." I replied as I sat down next to Michael.

"How do you know?" Josh asked. Everyone starred at me waiting for an answer.

"I just do." I said.

"You have been talking to him." Lexi said, reading my mind. "You gave Michael a phone when he left and you two been texting each other the entire time."

"Yes." I admitted. Everyone looked at me shocked.

"Why didn't you say anything? You have had us all thinking you've given up on him." Tony said.

"That was the plan." I said. Everyone looked at me with a blank expression on their faces. "After the last time we knew Derek would come back for him so Michael and I came up with a plan to get rid of Derek once and for all."

"As in you're going to kill him?" Josh asked.

"No, nothing like that." I said.

"So, what's the plan?" Charles asked.

"Nope." I said. "Not happening."

"What's not happening?" Tommy asked.

"I'm not telling any of you this plan." I said. I stood back up.

"Why not?" Tony asked. "We can help."

"That's why I'm not telling you the plan." I said. "Two people have died just for helping me. I don't want anyone else to get hurt."

"But Nicole-" Tommy started to say, but I put my hands up to stop him.

"I've made my decision." I said. I walked away without another word. I'm saving Michael and I'm saving him alone.

CHAPTER 12

Saving Michael

THE PLAN WAS supposed to be simple. I was just going to sneak out of the house while everyone was sleeping and drive to Jamestown alone. No one would know that I was leaving. When I got to Jamestown, Michael and I were going to come up with a plan to get rid of Derck for good that didn't involve killing anyone.

That simple plan didn't work out.

I was caught.

I almost had it. I was close. I was packed. I made sure I had enough gas to leave town. I was ready to go. I waited until it was dark and everyone was asleep to leave my room with my shoes in one hand and my bag in the other. I made it past the kitchen, but that was it. When I got to the dark living room almost to the door the lights suddenly came on. I turned to see everyone sitting on the furniture with Josh standing by the light switch. No one looked happy to see me.

"Hey, how's everyone doing?" I asked, trying to act like they didn't just catch me trying to leave.

"Save it Nicole." Charles said.

"We can't believe you were trying to leave in the middle of the night on your own." Josh said.

"You guys knew I was leaving so how was this any of a shocker to you?" I asked.

"You haven't listened to anything we've said." Tommy said. "Every time we try to say anything about you leaving alone you walk away before we can get anything we want to say out."

"Because I've heard you all enough." I said, getting frustrated. "You all think I'm making a mistake by doing this alone with only Michael and want me to let you all help."

"You need to let us help." Tommy said. "We can get rid of him together."

"No." I said.

"We have a better chance of getting rid of Derek together as a team." Josh said. "I know how bad you want Derek gone because I want him gone too."

"You betrayed us for Derek." I pointed out.

"He used me to get Michael." Josh said. "Once he got what he wanted I was nothing, but an employee to him and when I didn't do his bidding he had his men in guns beat me until I could no longer walk. You saw what I looked like when you came back for Michael."

"Please let us help." Charles said.

"No." I said again. Charles stood up.

"You leave us no choice Nicole. I'm sorry that I have to do this." Charles said. I looked at him confused. Before I could say anything, I felt something hit me hard on the back of my head. I fell to the ground before darkness took over and I passed out.

I woke up and I was sitting up in a chair or something and my face was against something hard. I tried to move my legs, but there wasn't any room. I opened my eyes to see that I'm in a van. I looked around to see everyone staring at me including Tommy who was looking at me through the rearview mirror from the driver's seat. My question, how did I get into the van?

"You're probably very confused right now." Carmen said. Caitlyn hasn't really said anything since Michael left so it wasn't surprising that she went from staring at me to staring out the window when her sister started talking.

"No, I've got an idea of what's going on." I said. "You all do realize kidnapping is illegal, right?"

"Yes, we're aware." Charles said. "But in our defense, we didn't have a choice."

"You did. You could have stayed out of it." I said.

"Too late for that." Tommy said. I looked out the window as the Welcome to Jamestown sign went by. I sat back in my seat.

"I can't believe you guys did this." I said. "When Derek sees us all there I'll be arrested once he calls and tells the police I'm there."

"He can call them all he wants. It won't matter." Carmen said. I looked at her. "Look around. Lexi isn't here." I looked. She was right. Lexi wasn't in the van.

"Where did she go?" I asked.

"Home. She called the police in New York City and I paid for a plane ticket. She already arrived at JFK and already had a meeting with the police so it shouldn't be long."

Everything went silent as we drove through Jamestown. People stared at the van as we drove by them. They all looked like they were scared. A goon did once tell me they needed to get Michael back so Derek would be nicer. Tommy drive to the last known place Derek held us. Jerry's house. Tommy pulled up to the end of the driveway and stopped. Derek's goons were scattered on the porch and in the yard. It looked to be about twenty men, maybe more. All of them had guns. Immediately I got out of the van and started up the driveway. I could hear shouts to come back, but I ignored them.

"What's up goons?" I said when I got close enough. I got their attention.

"IT'S HER!" they shouted and pointed their guns at me.

"Hey woah, is that necessary?" I asked.

"Wait until Derek finds out you actually had the nerve to show up. You won't be here long. One call and you're going to be on your way to jail for good." Nathan said, coming towards me.

"Oh, hey head goon. Long time no see." I said. "I'm guessing none of you heard. Lexi called herself and told the police everything and when I say everything I mean everything so you might want to get ahold of your boss." Nathan glared at me before disappearing into the house. No one else moved.

"Well, you've got some nerve showing up here." Derek said as he appeared onto the porch. "Stay there while I call the police. You make this way too easy." Derek went back into the house.

"So, none of you are going to tell him?" I asked. No one said anything or moved. A few minutes later Derek came storming back onto the porch. You could tell he was pissed. If he was a cartoon there would be fire shooting out of his head.

"SHE WENT BACK!" Derek shouted.

"So, you know." I said, smirking. "Gets worse for you too."

"How?" Derek asked, walking off the porch. "How is it going to get worse for me?"

"Lexi won't be lying when they ask her what happened to her." I said.

"She better if she knows what is good for her." Derek warned.

"What are you going to do Derek?" I asked. "She's all the way in New York City surrounded by police officers."

"Then it's not going to get worse for me because they can't touch me." Derek said. "This isn't in their derestriction."

"Do you know how things work?" I asked. "This might not be in their derestriction, but they call the ones that are."

"None of the ones here are going to arrest me." Derek said.

"Probably not, but I'm sure they have called the FBI by now and I'm sure they won't have a problem doing it." I said.

"Get her!" Derek ordered. No one moved. "What the hell are you morons waiting for? An invitation? I SAID GET HER!" Everyone moved at once and I was grabbed. They pushed me past Derek and into the house. Everything looked so different. All of Jerry's furniture was removed and replaced with the furniture of Derek and Michael's childhood home. Whichever goon that had me pushed me forward. We went up the steps and I was pushed to the door at the end of the hall. They knocked once before opening then pushed me in and shutting the door leaving me in the room. Before I could make a move, I heard a book close behind me, making me jump and turn around quickly.

"You're late." Michael said. "You were supposed to be here two days ago."

"Not my fault. I was all set to go and as I was leaving I got hit behind the head and was knocked out." I said.

"Damn. Well, since you were late I've had time to think of a plan and I have to say this plan is pretty good." Michael said, patting the seat next to him for me to join him.

"This out to be good." I said, sitting next to Michael.

"Well, I made sure they didn't find the phone you gave me when I left with Derek every time they search me and I recorded Derek a few times." Michael said.

"Doing what?" I asked.

"Doing what Derek does. Making threats, making me lift people when they don't cooperate." Michael said. "And just yesterday he killed someone."

"HE WHAT?!" I shouted. Michael quickly covered my mouth.

"Keep your voice down!" Michael said. "They hear you and they will come in and see what you're shouting about and we will get caught."

"Michael, who did he kill? And please tell me you got it on video." I said.

"His name was Jordan. He was a guy that owed Derek a lot of money and hasn't made any interest in paying him back." Michael said, grabbing the phone from someplace I didn't see. "Derek used him as an example on what not to do."

"What happened?" I asked.

"See for yourself." Michael said. He handed me the phone. It was on a video and I pressed play. The video started playing. The first thing I saw was Derek. He was surrounded by his goons and some other people. Most of his goons were pointing a gun at someone. Derek was walking around someone that seemed to be tied up from behind and was on his knees.

"So," Derek began. "Some of you seem to think you can pull a fast one on me. You think you can just take money from me and not pay me back."

"No Derek," the guy on the ground said. "No one thinks that."

"That's Jordan." Michael said, pointing to the guy on the ground.

"I got that." I said, going back to the video.

"Every time payment is due you avoid my men and my brother." Derek said.

"I'm sorry. It won't happen again. I won't avoid them ever again." Jordan said.

"Payments were due yesterday." Derek said. Jordan looked down at the ground. "Do you have my money to pay back?"

"No." Jordan said in a very low voice.

"I can't hear you." Derek said "Do you have money to give me?"

"No." Jordan said louder.

"I am very disappointed in you Jordan." Derek said. "I didn't want to do this, but you've left me no choice."

"Derek please, I have a family. A wife and kids." Jordan pleaded. I watched as Derek pulled something out.

"Is that a whip?" I asked Michael.

"Yeah it is. He got it specifically for this." Michael said. I didn't say anything back. I just went back to the video.

"Derek please don't do this. I promise, I'll get you your money." Jordan pleaded.

"This is going to hurt me a lot more than it's going to hurt you." Derek said as he walked behind Jordan.

"Really?" Jordan asked.

"No, this is going to hurt just you." Derek said. He started to whip Jordan's back. Jordan screamed out in pain as the whip hit his back. Everyone around them turned their heads away as Derek hit him with the whip over and over again.

"How many times does he hit him?" I asked. I don't know how much more I can watch.

"It ends soon." Michael said. I just nodded.

"Derek enough," Nathan said, coming forward and taking the whip out of Derek's hands. "He's had enough."

"I'll tell you when he's had enough!" Derek said. He pushed Nathan back. "I want everyone to see what happens when you double cross me and do not pay me back." Derek said. He pulled a gun out of the back of his pants and aimed it at Jordan. Without hesitating Derek pulled the trigger and Jordan fell to the ground.

"Did he suffer?" I asked.

"Not after the whipping. He died instantly." Michael said. I sighed in relief before opening a new text and sending the video. "Who did you send that to?"

"Lexi." I said. "She went back to New York City and is with the police right now."

"I thought she was still with you." Michael said. "Wasn't it the others that hit you on the head?"

"She was with us when they hit me in the head and knocked me out." I said. "But when I came to I was already in the van coming into Jamestown and Lexi was gone."

"Does Derek know?" Michael asked.

"That he can no longer call the police to stop me. Yes. I got pushed into the room after he found out." I said.

"Where are the others?" Michael asked.

"They are-" I stopped talking when the door slammed open and all the others were pushed in. Derek came in after them. "Right here."

"I thought you two might have been missing your friends." Derek said. "I'll let you all get acquainted. My men will be back shortly for your execution. Since I can't get rid of you by sending you to jail, I'll just get rid of you by killing you." Derek left without another word, shutting the door behind him.

We have been in the room together for more than an hour and no one has said a word. Charles was holding the twins with Tommy standing in front of them. Josh and Tony were on the other side not saying a word, just sitting together. Michael and I have been in the same spot since I sat down next to him.

"Guys listen up." I said. "I have something to say before the goons come for us."

"Nicole, you don't have to say anything." Charles said. Everyone nodded as they agreed with Charles.

"No, I need to say this." I said. "I never meant for any of this to happen. This was not what I wanted to be doing. I didn't even think any of this would happen. I'm so glad that Ethan decided to kick me out of his life and I wish all of you did the first time we had any trouble."

"Nicole-" Charles tried to start, but I stopped him.

"Please let me finish." I said. He nodded. "Knowing you all has been the greatest thing about all of this and I am so sorry about the way it's ending." The door slammed open. A few goons came in and pointed their guns at us.

"Times up. Everyone is waiting for you." One of them said. He looked at me. "Time to die." He motioned us all forward with his gun and we all walked out of the room.

"Nicole wait," I heart Tommy said. I was spun around and instantly felt a pair of warm lips on mine. Without hesitation I kissed him back.

"Enough! Get a move on! It's execution time!" someone said., We broke apart from the kid and continued to leave the house. We got outside and everyone was standing in the yard in a giant circle with Derek in the middle. We walked into the middle of the circle and immediately all our hands were bound behind our backs.

"This didn't have to end this way you know." Derek said. "You could have just left us alone from the beginning and no one would be dying tonight."

"No one still has to die tonight." I said.

"Oh yes they do." Derek said. He walked over to Michael. "You, I took care of you when you killed our parents. I made sure no one arrested you for it and I took care of you and this is the thanks I get."

"You turned me into your own money mule and had me throwing people when they did something you didn't like. That's not something I wanted to do." Michael said.

"Better me then someone else." Derek said. He went to Josh. "You were my best friend."

"You had people lock me up so I wouldn't tell anyone what you were doing to your brother." Josh said.

"Well, I didn't want you telling people what he did. Then they would have known and my plan to use him would have been ruined." Derek said. "Besides, take that as a compliment. I wanted to kill you all those years and now I am."

"Derek wait!" I said. He walked over and stood in front of me. "You don't need to kill anyone. Just me. I am the reason for all of this. I didn't mind my own business when I was told to. I dragged everyone into this and none of them deserve to die because of my mistake, because I wouldn't listen to what I was told."

"Why should I spare their lives?" Derek asked. "None of them matter to me."

"They are just kids. They don't deserve to die." I said, gesturing to Michael, Tony, Carmen, and Caitlyn.

"What about the rest?" Derek asked. No one said anything. "You know what? You're right. They don't deserve to die, but not because they are young. But because I can use their powers and no one will ever betray me again. The rest of you, I don't need."

"I'm all the girls have left." Charles said.

"We are all the girls have left." Tommy corrected Charles.

"Not my problem." Derek said. He pointed the gun at me. "And I'm going to start with one that has caused me the most problems." Derek pointed his gun at me with his finger on the trigger. I closed my eyes waiting to hear the pop before the bullet will hit me, but before he pulled the trigger I heard something coming close.

Sirens.

All the goons scattered as Derek just stood there. He looked shocked as many police cars came in blocking everyone from leaving. A SWAT truck pulled up.

"Put the guns down and put your hands above your head." Someone said through a bullhorn. All the goons dropped their guns to their feet, putting their hands up in the air to surrender. Derek didn't move as police officers came up behind each goon and arrested them.

"You are all pathetic!" Derek shouted.

"Put the gun own and put your hands above your head." A police officer said as around twenty officers surrounded all of us with their guns pointed at Derek.

"NICOLE!" Lexi shouted. She pushed past the officers and started untying all of us.

"It's over Derek. Put the gun down." The officer said. Derek looked around and then dropped the gun. He was tackled to the ground and put in handcuffs.

"This isn't over! I'll be back for all of you!" Derek shouted.

"Shut up!" an officer said. We stood there together and watched as Derek and all of his goons were put in the back of police cars and trucks. As the cars all pulled away Michael spoke.

"So, what now?"

CPSIA information can be obtained
at www.ICGtesting.com
Printed in the USA
BVHW070943110319
542311BV00008B/185/P